Terror on a Dead World

We were approaching the side flight of steps that led up to the vaulted entrance of the great tower. We moved by now in a kind of daze, crushed as we were by the terrific psychic attack that was rapidly conquering our courage.

Then came the climax. The lofty doors of the tower swung slowly open. And from within the building there lurched and shambled out a thing, the sight of which froze us where we stood.

"*That* never came from any part of our own galaxy!" Dril cried hoarsely.

It was black, mountainous in bulk and of a shape that tore the brain with horror. It was something like a monstrous, squatting toad, its flesh a heaving black slime from which protruded sticky black limbs that were not quite either tentacles or arms.

Its triangle of eyes were three slits of cold green fire that watched us with hypnotic intensity. Beneath that hideous chinless face its breathing pouch swelled in and out painfully as it lurched, slobbering, down the steps toward us.

Other Avon Camelot Books
Compiled and Edited by
Bruce Coville

BRUCE COVILLE'S ALIEN VISITORS
BRUCE COVILLE'S SHAPESHIFTERS

Coming Soon

BRUCE COVILLE'S UFOs

BRUCE COVILLE'S
STRANGE WORLDS

COMPILED AND EDITED BY
BRUCE COVILLE

ASSISTED BY STEVEN ROMAN

Illustrated by Ernie Colón and John Nyberg

A GLC BOOK

AN AVON CAMELOT BOOK

AVON BOOKS, INC.
1350 Avenue of the Americas
New York, New York 10019

Copyright © 2000 by General Licensing Company, Inc. All rights reserved.
Cover artwork copyright © 2000 by General Licensing Company, Inc.
Cover painting by Ernie Colón
Illustrations by Ernie Colón and John Nyberg

Introduction copyright © 1999 by Bruce Coville.
"A Walk in the Dark" copyright © 1950 by Arthur C. Clarke; originally published in *Thrilling Wonder Stories* (August 1950). Reprinted by permission of the author and author's agents, Scovil Chichak Galen Literary Agency, Inc., New York.
"Healer" copyright © 1999 by Connie Wilkins.
"2064, or Thereabouts" copyright © 1992 by David R. Bunch; first published in *Fantastic*, 1964. Reprinted by permission of the author.
"The Looking Glass" copyright © 1999 by Alethea Eason.
"Free Will" copyright © 1999 by John C. Bunnell.
"Egg Shells" copyright © 1999 by Nina Kiriki Hoffman.
"Cockfight" copyright © 1993 by Jane Yolen. First published by Ace in *Dragons of Light,* Orson Scott Card, ed. Now appears in *Here There Be Dragons* by Jane Yolen, published by Harcourt Brace and Company, 1993. Reprinted by permission of Curtis Brown, Ltd.
"Hello, Darling" copyright © 1996 by Anne Mazer. Reprinted by permission of Anne Mazer from *A Sliver of Glass and Other Uncommon Tales.* All rights reserved.
"Trading Places" copyright © 1999 by Noreen Doyle.
"The Sea Turned Upside Down" copyright © 1999 by Gus Grenfell.
"Whoooo-ooo Flupper!" copyright © 1986 by Nicholas Fisk.
"The Dead Planet" copyright © 1949 by Edmond Hamilton. Reprinted by permission of the author's Estate and the agent for the Estate, Eleanor Wood.
"Fun on Phrominium" copyright © 1999 by Karen Jordan Allen.
"Sweet Home" copyright © 1999 by Nancy Varian Berberick.

Library of Congress Catalog Card Number: 98-94952
ISBN: 0-380-80256-2
www.avonbooks.com

First Avon Camelot Printing: February 2000

CAMELOT TRADEMARK REG. U.S. PAT. OFF. AND IN OTHER COUNTRIES, MARCA REGISTRADA, HECHO EN U.S.A.

Printed in the U.S.A.

OPM 10 9 8 7 6 5 4 3 2 1

CONTENTS

INTRODUCTION:

Welcome . . . Stranger

From the time humans first lifted their heads to look at a distant horizon, we have taken delight in wondering what was just out of sight, just beyond reach. For thousands of years we have daydreamed about faraway cities, strange and exotic; about dense and unknown jungles; about lost civilizations and hidden treasure.

But something strange, something brand new, has happened to us Earthlings in the last decade or so.

We've run out of unknown places.

As our world is stitched ever more closely together by jet planes, satellite links, and the Internet—as distance sheds its meaning—we're losing the sense that it might be possible to go someplace no one has ever been before, at least not for hundreds, or even thousands of years. Sure, there are still mountains to climb. But even if you get to the top of Mount Everest, you'll know someone's been there before you. And while Africa may not have been mapped down to the last inch, the odds of finding a great lost city there (as Tarzan used to do every book or so) seem considerably lower than they used to.

All this leaves an empty spot in the human heart—a spot hungry not for answers, but for mystery. A spot that longs for the unknown, the unmapped, the uncharted. We yearn for dragons in a world too small to hold them.

It's not as if most of us would ever actually journey to those unknown places even if they still existed. But the *possibility* of them—the knowledge that you *could* go someplace strange and unknown—has always been important to our hearts. The sense that that possibility is vanishing leaves us with an itch that can only be scratched by a certain kind of science fiction—the kind you'll find in the stories that follow. Tales in which the authors carry us to strange new worlds—worlds where much may be known, but even more remains a mystery.

So, welcome aboard the good ship *Weird*. You're just in time to blast off for some truly odd adventures.

Just remember to stay with the group so you don't get lost.

Oh, what's the use of telling *you* that? It's clear you're the type who's bound and determined to stray from the path so you can go looking for something strange and new.

Ah, well. That's what exploring is all about.

But remember this: We truly don't know what's waiting out there, on all those billions of distant planets and strange worlds.

Most of it is still a mystery.

Thank goodness.

A Walk in the Dark

by Arthur C. Clarke

Robert Armstrong had walked just over two miles, as far as he could judge, when his torch failed. He stood still for a moment, unable to believe that such a misfortune could really have befallen him. Then, half maddened with rage, he hurled the useless instrument away. It landed somewhere in the darkness, disturbing the silence of this little world. A metallic echo came ringing back from the low hills: then all was quiet again.

This, thought Armstrong, was the ultimate misfortune. Nothing more could happen to him now. He was never able to laugh bitterly at his luck, and resolved never again to imagine that the fickle goddess had ever favored him. Who would have believed that the only tractor at Camp IV would have broken down when he was just setting off for Port Sanderson? He recalled the frenzied repair work, the relief when the second start had been made—and the final debacle when the caterpillar track had jammed.

It was no use, then, regretting the lateness of his departure: he could not have foreseen these accidents, and it was still a good four hours before the *Canopus* took off. He *had* to catch her, whatever happened; no other ship would be touching at this world for another month.

2

Apart from the urgency of his business, four more weeks on this out-of-the-way planet were unthinkable.

There had been only one thing to do. It was lucky that Port Sanderson was little more than six miles from the camp—not a great distance, even on foot. He had to leave all his equipment behind, but it could follow on the next ship and he could manage without it. The road was poor, merely stamped out of the rock by one of the Board's hundred-ton crushers, but there was no fear of going astray.

Even now, he was in no real danger, though he might well be too late to catch the ship. Progress would be slow, for he dare not risk losing the road in this region of canyons and enigmatic tunnels that had never been explored. It was, of course, pitch-dark. Here at the edge of the galaxy the stars were so few and scattered that their light was negligible. The strange crimson sun of this lonely world would not rise for many hours, and although five of the little moons were in the sky they could barely be seen by the unaided eye. Not one of them could even cast a shadow.

Armstrong was not a man to bewail his luck for long. He began to walk slowly along the road, feeling its texture with his feet. It was, he knew, fairly straight except where it wound through Carver's Pass. He wished he had a stick or something to probe the way before him, but he would have to rely for guidance on the feel of the ground.

It was terribly slow at first, until he gained confidence. He had never known how difficult it was to

3

walk in a straight line. Although the feeble stars gave him his bearings, again and again he found himself stumbling among the virgin rocks at the edge of the crude roadway. He was traveling in long zigzags that took him to alternate sides of the road. Then he would stub his toes against the bare rock and grope his way back on to the hard-packed surface once again.

Presently it settled down to a routine. It was impossible to estimate his speed; he could only struggle along and hope for the best. There were four miles to go—four miles and as many hours. It should be easy enough, unless he lost his way. But he dared not think of that.

Once he had mastered the technique he could afford the luxury of thought. He could not pretend that he was enjoying the experience, but he had been in much worse positions before. As long as he remained on the road, he was perfectly safe. He had been hoping that as his eyes became adapted to the starlight he would be able to see the way, but he now knew that the whole journey would be blind. The discovery gave him a vivid sense of his remoteness from the heart of the galaxy. On a night as clear as this, the skies of almost any other planet would have been blazing with stars. Here at this outpost of the universe the sky held perhaps a hundred faintly gleaming points of light, as useless as the five ridiculous moons on which no one had ever bothered to land.

A slight change in the road interrupted his thoughts. Was there a curve here, or had he veered off

4

to the right again? He moved very slowly along the invisible and ill-defined border. Yes, there was no mistake: the road was bending to the left. He tried to remember its appearance in the daytime, but he had only seen it once before. Did this mean that he was nearing the pass? He hoped so, for the journey would then be half completed.

He peered ahead into the blackness, but the ragged line of the horizon told him nothing. Presently he found that the road had straightened itself again and his spirits sank. The entrance to the pass must still be some way ahead: there were at least four miles to go.

Four miles—how ridiculous the distance seemed! How long would it take the *Canopus* to travel four miles? He doubted if man could measure so short an interval of time. And how many trillions of miles had he, Robert Armstrong, traveled in his life? It must have reached a staggering total by now, for in the last twenty years he had scarcely stayed more than a month at a time on any single world. This very year, he had twice made the crossing of the galaxy, and that was a notable journey even in these days of the phantom drive.

He tripped over a loose stone, and the jolt brought him back to reality. It was no use, here, thinking of ships that could eat up the light-years. He was facing nature, with no weapons but his own strength and skill.

It was strange that it took him so long to identify the real cause of his uneasiness. The last four weeks had been very full, and the rush of his departure, coupled with the annoyance and anxiety caused by the tractor's breakdowns, had driven everything else from his mind. Moreover, he had always prided himself on his hardheadedness and lack of imagination. Until now, he had forgotten all about that first evening at the base, when the crews had regaled him with the usual tall yarns concocted for the benefit of newcomers.

It was then that the old base clerk had told the story of his walk by night from Port Sanderson to the camp, and of what had trailed him through Carver's Pass, keeping always beyond the limit of his torchlight. Armstrong, who had heard such tales on a score of worlds, had paid it little attention at the time. This planet, after all, was known to be uninhabited. But logic could not dispose of the matter as easily as that. Suppose, after all, there was some truth in the old man's fantastic tale . . . ?

It was not a pleasant thought, and Armstrong did not intend to brood upon it. But he knew that if he dismissed it out of hand it would continue to prey on his mind. The only way to conquer imaginary fears was to face them boldly; he would have to do that now.

His strongest argument was the complete barrenness of this world and its utter desolation, though against that one could set many counter-arguments, as indeed the old clerk had done. Man had only lived on this planet for twenty years, and much of it was still unexplored. No one could deny that the tunnels out in the wasteland were rather puzzling, but everyone believed them to be volcanic vents. Though, of course, life often crept into such places. With a shudder he remembered the giant polyps that had snared the first explorers of Vargon III.

It was all very inconclusive. Suppose, for the sake of argument, one granted the existence of life here. What of that?

The vast majority of life forms in the universe were completely indifferent to man. Some, of course, like the gas-beings of Alcoran or the roving wave-lattices of Shandaloon, could not even detect him but passed through or around him as if he did not exist. Others were merely inquisitive, some embarrassingly friendly. There were few indeed that would attack unless provoked.

Nevertheless, it was a grim picture that the old stores clerk had painted. Back in the warm, well-lighted smoking room, with the drinks going around, it had been easy enough to laugh at it. But here in the darkness, miles from any human settlement, it was very different.

It was almost a relief when he stumbled off the road again and had to grope with his hands until he found it once more. This seemed a very rough patch, and the road was scarcely distinguishable from the rocks around. In a few minutes, however, he was safely on his way again.

It was unpleasant to see how quickly his thoughts returned to the same disquieting subject. Clearly it was worrying him more than he cared to admit.

He drew consolation from one fact: it had been quite obvious that no one at the Base had believed the old fellow's story. Their questions and banter had proved that. At the time, he had laughed as loudly as any of them. After all, what *was* the evidence? A dim shape, just seen in the darkness, that might well have been an oddly formed rock. And the curious clicking noise that had so impressed the old man—anyone could imagine such sounds at night if they were sufficiently over-wrought. If it had been hostile, why hadn't the creature come any closer? "Because it was afraid of my light," the old chap had said. Well, that was plausible enough: it would explain why nothing had ever been seen in the daylight. Such a creature might live underground, only emerging at night—darn it! Armstrong got control of his thoughts again. If he went on this way, he told himself angrily, he would soon be seeing and hearing a whole menagerie of monsters.

There was, of course, one factor that disposed of the ridiculous story at once. It was really very simple; he felt sorry he hadn't thought of it before. *What would such a creature live on?* There was not even a trace of vegetation on the whole planet. He laughed to think that the bogey could be disposed of so easily—and in the same instant felt annoyed with himself for not laughing aloud. If he was so sure of his reasoning, why not whistle, or sing, or do anything to keep up his spirits? He put the question fairly to himself as a test of his manhood. Half-ashamed, he had to admit that he was still afraid—afraid because "there *might* be something in it, after all." But at least his analysis had done him some good.

It would have been better if he had left it there, and remained half-convinced by his argument. But a part of his mind was still busily trying to break down his careful reasoning. It succeeded only too well, and when he remembered the plant-beings of Xantil Major the shock was so unpleasant that he stopped dead in his tracks.

Now, the plant-beings of Xantil were not in any way horrible. They were in fact extremely beautiful creatures. But what made them appear so distressing now was the knowledge that they could live for indefinite periods with no food whatsoever. All the energy they needed for their strange lives they extracted from cosmic radiation—and that was almost as intense here as anywhere else in the universe.

He had scarcely thought of one example before others crowded into his mind and he remembered the life form on Trantor Beta, which was the only one known capable of directly utilizing atomic energy. That too had lived on an utterly barren world, very much like this . . .

Armstrong's mind was rapidly splitting into two distinct portions, each trying to convince the other and neither wholly succeeding. He did not realize how far his morale had gone until he found himself holding his breath lest it conceal any sound from the darkness about him. Angrily, he cleared his mind of the rubbish that had been gathering there and turned once more to the immediate problem.

There was no doubt that the road was slowly rising, and the silhouette of the horizon seemed much higher in the sky. The road began to twist, and suddenly he was aware of great rocks on either side of him. Soon only a narrow ribbon of sky was still visible, and the darkness became, if possible, even more intense.

Somehow, he felt safer with the rock walls surrounding him: it meant that he was protected except in two directions. Also, the road had been leveled more carefully and it was easy to keep to it. Best of all, he knew now that the journey was more than half completed.

For a moment his spirits began to rise. Then, with maddening perversity, his mind went back into the old grooves again. He remembered that it was on the far side of Carver's Pass that the old clerk's adventure had taken place—if it had ever happened at all.

In half a mile, he would be out in the open again, out of the protection of these sheltering rocks. The thought seemed doubly horrible now and he already felt a sense of nakedness. He could be attacked from any direction, and he would be utterly helpless . . .

Until now, he had still retained some self-control. Very resolutely he had kept his mind away from the one fact that gave some color to the old man's tale—the single piece of evidence that had stopped the banter in the crowded room back at the camp and brought a sudden hush upon the company. Now, as Armstrong's will weakened, he recalled again the words that had struck a momentary chill even in the warm comfort of the Base building.

The little clerk had been very insistent on one point. He had never heard any sound of pursuit from the dim shape sensed, rather than seen, at the limit of his light. There was no scuffling of claws or hoofs on rock, nor even the clatter of displaced stones. It was as if, so the old man had declared in that solemn manner of his, "as if the thing that was following could see perfectly in the darkness, and had many small legs or pads so that it could move swiftly and easily over the rock—like a giant caterpillar or one of the carpet-things of Kralkor II."

Yet, although there had been no noise of pursuit, there had been one sound that the old man had caught several times. It was so unusual that its very strangeness made it doubly ominous. It was the faint but horribly persistent *clicking*.

The old fellow had been able to describe it very vividly—too vividly for Armstrong's liking now.

"Have you ever listened to a large insect crunching its prey?" he said. "Well, it was just like that. I imagine that a crab makes exactly the same noise with its claws when it clashes them together. It was a—what's the word?—a *chitinous* sound."

At this point, Armstrong remembered laughing loudly. (Strange, how it was all coming back to him now.) But no one else had laughed, though they had been quick to do so earlier. Sensing the change of tone, he had sobered at once and asked the old man to continue his story. How he wished now that he had stifled his curiosity!

It had been quickly told. The next day, a party of skeptical technicians had gone into the no-man's-land beyond Carver's Pass. They were not skeptical enough to leave their guns behind, but they had no cause to use them, for they found no trace of any living thing. There were the inevitable pits and tunnels, glistening holes down which the light of the torches rebounded endlessly until it was lost in the distance—but the planet was riddled with them.

Though the party found no sign of life, it discovered one thing it did not like at all. Out in the barren and unexplored land beyond the pass they had come upon an even larger tunnel than the rest. Near the mouth of that tunnel was a massive rock, half embedded in the ground. And the sides of that rock had been worn away *as if it had been used as an enormous whetstone*.

No fewer than five of those present had seen this disturbing rock. None of them could explain it satisfactorily as a natural formation, but they still refused to accept the old man's story. Armstrong had asked them if they had ever put it to the test. There had been an uncomfortable silence. Then big Hargraves had said: "Hell, who'd walk out to the pass at night just for fun!" and had left it at that. Indeed, there was no other record of anyone walking from Port Sanderson to the camp by night, or for that matter by day. During the hours of light, no unprotected human being could live in the open beneath the rays of the enormous, lurid sun that seemed to fill half the sky. And no one would walk six miles, wearing radiation armor, if the tractor was available.

Armstrong felt that he was leaving the pass. The rocks on either side were falling away, and the road was no longer as firm and well-caked as it had been. He was coming out into the open plain once more, and somewhere not far away in the darkness was that enigmatic pillar that might have been used for sharpening monstrous fangs or claws. It was not a reassuring thought, but he could not get it out of his mind.

Feeling distinctly worried now, Armstrong made a great effort to pull himself together. He would try to be rational again; he would think of business, the work he had done at camp—anything but this infernal place. For a while, he succeeded quite well. But presently, with a maddening persistence, every train of thought came back to the same point. He could not get out of his mind the picture of that inexplicable rock and its appalling possibilities. Over and over again he found himself wondering how far away it was, whether he had already passed it, and whether it was on his right or his left . . .

The ground was quite flat again, and the road drove on straight as an arrow. There was one gleam of consolation: Port Sanderson could not be much more than two miles away. Armstrong had no idea how long he had been on the road. Unfortunately, his watch was not illuminated and he could only guess at the passage of time. With any luck, the *Canopus* should not take off for another two hours at least. But he could not be sure, and now another fear began to enter his head— the dread that he might see a vast constellation of lights rising swiftly into the sky ahead, and know that all this agony of mind had been in vain.

He was not zigzagging so badly now, and seemed to

be able to anticipate the edge of the road before stumbling off it. It was probable, he cheered himself by thinking, that he was traveling almost as fast as if he had a light. If all went well, he might be nearing Port Sanderson in thirty minutes—a ridiculously small space of time. How he would laugh at his fears when he strolled into his already reserved stateroom in the *Canopus*, and felt that peculiar quiver as the phantom drive hurled the great ship far out of this system, back to the clustered starclouds near the center of the galaxy— back toward Earth itself, which he had not seen for so many years. One day, he told himself, he really must visit Earth again. All his life he had been making the promise, but always there had been the same answer— lack of time. Strange, wasn't it, that such a tiny planet should have played so enormous a part in the development of the universe, should even have come to dominate worlds far wiser and more intelligent than itself!

Armstrong's thoughts were harmless again, and he felt calmer. The knowledge that he was nearing Port Sanderson was immensely reassuring, and he deliberately kept his mind on familiar, unimportant matters. Carver's Pass was already far behind, and with it that thing he no longer intended to recall. One day, if he ever returned to this world, he would visit the pass in the daytime and laugh at his fears. In twenty minutes now, they would have joined the nightmares of his childhood.

It was almost a shock, though one of the most pleasant he had ever known, when he saw the lights of Port Sanderson come up over the horizon. The curvature of this little world was very deceptive: it did not seem right that a planet with a gravity almost as great as Earth's should have a horizon so close at hand. One day, someone would have to discover what lay at this world's core to give it so great a density. Perhaps the many tunnels would help—it was an unfortunate turn of thought, but the nearness of his goal had robbed it of terror now. Indeed, the thought that he might really be in danger seemed to give his adventure a certain piquancy and heightened interest. Nothing could happen to him now, with ten minutes to go and the lights of the port already in sight.

A few minutes later, his feelings changed abruptly when he came to the sudden bend in the road. He had forgotten the chasm that caused his detour and added half a mile to the journey. *Well, what of it*? he thought stubbornly. An extra half-mile would make no difference now—another ten minutes, at the most.

It was very disappointing when the lights of the city vanished. Armstrong had not remembered the hill that the road was skirting; perhaps it was only a low ridge, scarcely noticeable in the daytime. But by hiding the lights of the port it had taken away his chief talisman and left him again at the mercy of his fears.

Very unreasonably, his intelligence told him, he began to think how horrible it would be if anything happened now, so near the end of the journey. He kept the worst of his fears at bay for a while, hoping desperately that the lights of the city would soon reappear. But as the minutes dragged on, he realized that the ridge must be longer than he imagined. He tried to

15

cheer himself by the thought that the city would be all the nearer when he saw it again, but somehow logic seemed to have failed him now. For presently he found himself doing something he had not stooped to, even out in the waste by Carver's Pass.

He stopped, turned slowly round, and with bated breath listened until his lungs were nearly bursting.

The silence was uncanny, considering how near he must be to the port. There was certainly no sound from behind him. Of course there wouldn't be, he told himself angrily. But he was immensely relieved. The thought of that faint and insistent clicking had been haunting him for the last hour.

So friendly and familiar was the noise that did reach him at last that the anticlimax almost made him laugh aloud. Drifting through the still air from a source clearly not more than a mile away came the sound of a landing-field tractor, perhaps one of the machines loading the *Canopus* itself. In a matter of seconds, thought Armstrong, he would be around this ridge with the port only a few hundred yards ahead. The journey was nearly ended. In a few moments, this evil plain would be no more than a fading nightmare.

It seemed terribly unfair: so little time, such a small fraction of a human life, was all he needed now. But the gods have always been unfair to man, and now they were enjoying their little jest. For there could be no mistaking the rattle of monstrous claws in the darkness *ahead of him*.

HEALER

by Connie Wilkins

The sun was a golden fur-fruit in the orange sky, its disk the clearest Jule had seen in half a year. The winds on the surface must have really died down, she thought, as she watched the shadow of her wings slide lazily down the redrock cliffs.

If she ever went off-world, would she long for this sky the way Marra dreamed of Earth's blue heaven? It was hard to imagine.

This might have been a good day to hunt for lichens up above, with airborne dust at a minimum and the roar of the wind-powered electric turbines quieted. But it was also a beautiful day for soaring in the Rift, and she didn't regret her choice.

Getting back home might be tricky, though, with the change in air currents. On the other hand, clearer air would mean more sunlight far below, which would mean new thermal updrafts, and nobody was better than Jule at finding and riding thermals.

Nobody was better at spotting green, either.

"Over this way, Bili," she called into the com on her shoulder. "Where the rock juts out like a Klytyk's beak." She glanced to the west to see his long slender wings bank and veer and glide toward her. "There's a ledge under the overhang. I think we can get a foothold."

There was more than just a ledge beneath the jutting

rock. A cave, almost hidden by the gray-green fans of eye-weed, extended deeper into the cliff than her sun-dazzled eyes could see.

As her feet touched stone she pulled the cord to re-tract her wings. Bili's shadow brushed her as he sailed past, not quite close enough to land; then he was too low to make it on this pass.

"Catch you after you hop an updraft," Jule called.

His voice crackled in her earphones as she slipped out of her wing harness. "You could have caught me this time if you'd been paying attention!"

"Sorry!" Jule was already ducking her head and moving into the beckoning darkness. It would take ten or fifteen minutes for Bili to get back. It had been nice of him to use his vacation from construction-track to help her hunt for medicinal plants, but the idea of a little solitary exploration appealed to her. Soon enough she too would be condemned to school in Rift City, study-ing the tech side of healer-track, stifling in the crowds and heavy air two miles below.

Thick, fleshy leaves clung to the overhang and the roof of the cave. Dozens of white-rimmed black "eyes" stood out along their edges, turning toward Jule as she stooped and slipped past. She knew they were trig-gered by moisture, not light. As long as she kept mov-ing there was no danger, but stand still for more than five minutes and tiny rootlets would reach out, pene-trate even her leather coveralls, and draw out all the fluids in her body.

She didn't blame them. They were only trying to

survive, and anyway, what she had in mind for them was just as bad. What she had in mind first, though, was to see what else the cave might hold.

The eye-weeds grew sparser and paler as she moved inward. They ceased altogether where the ceiling sloped up enough to let her stand erect. As her eyes adjusted to the dimness she thought at first that there was only a single spacious cavern, but a barely perceptible glow at the back drew her on.

It was a good thing she stepped carefully. Even so, she had to scramble suddenly backward to keep from falling through the gap. She sat down hard on the rocky floor, but rolled to her knees right away and approached the edge of the hole at a cautious crawl.

Jewelmoss! She had hardly dared to hope, but there they were, patches of flickering colors, violet and crimson and gold and blue-green. Not pure mineral, not quite plant, they existed on no other known planet, and their beauty and rarity made them valuable to collectors. Just a few would earn enough credit from off-world traders to buy anything she wanted . . . like motorized wings for Marra. . . .

The smell of blood and pain cut through her elation. Not human blood—even an apprentice healer could tell that—but something she should recognize.

There was a shuffling movement far below, and a thin whistling sound like air escaping through a narrow opening. Or through tiny vents in hard shell. . . .

Jule knew before her lightrod was free of her belt what its beam would show.

She had seldom seen Klytyks close up, but often enough from a distance, their huge clawed forms black against the redrock of the mines. Marra told stories of being watched by wild ones in the early years as she searched for useful plants, and being led by them to some valuable finds, but these days it was dangerous for even such a noted healer to claim they were intelligent. Not that that always stopped her. Jule made it a point to know as little as possible about her grandmother's secret contacts with anti-slavery groups.

The light beam traveled past the clumps of jewelmoss clustered just under the lip of the hole. The rock was only three feet thick here, opening out into a lower cavern, but all Jule could see through the gap was an expanse of shiny black shell several feet below the rock.

The creature was stone still now, probably hoping not to be seen. Jule angled the light as much as she could and finally found the source of the blood smell and the waves of pain her healer training detected.

This Klytyk was slave, not wild; escaped slave, in fact. The implant that let the miners control it with agonizing jolts of electricity had been smashed, whether by accidental rockfall or deliberate act of courage, and with it a section of shell had splintered and partially peeled away.

Jule couldn't imagine how the creature had gotten here, but it was clear it could go no farther. A shard of carapace had worked its way down into the pink flesh like a spear, and orange blood tinged green with infection oozed out around the wound.

Healer instinct kicked in before any thought of consequences. Jule crossed back to the cave entrance in three bounds and tore at the first thick eye-weed leaves she found. She didn't realize Bili had landed until he called out in disgust, "Not that foul stuff! I can't stand to think about it, never mind touch it!"

She dropped the leaves and moved out onto the ledge. "I know what you mean, but it's a great find. You'll be glad enough of the juice next time you get hurt."

"I suppose, and in construction it's not a matter of 'if' but 'when.'" He sounded half proud of that, but she let it pass.

"You don't have to touch it. Just stay there and I'll give you a load to fly back to the plateau. Marra will take it from there." She pulled a net from her pack as she spoke and spread it on the ledge, not allowing herself to wonder why she didn't tell him what she'd found inside. His uncle was on the Council in Rift City; he'd know what to do about an escaped Klytyk. She really should tell. . . .

"I can do it if you can," Bili said grimly, and started to help her load the net, shaking his hands in disgust as he tossed in each leaf. "Don't think I'm getting soft just because I have to hang out with those air-suckers down below."

"Marra's an air-sucker and she's not soft," Jule said, for the sake of argument and to keep him from asking questions she wasn't ready to answer.

"That's different. She was born where there was lots

more air and more gravity, and she still doesn't use the oxygen tanks as much as some of those . . . those fur-fruits when they have to come up here."

"It's all in what you're used to," Jule said, knowing what was really bothering him. Some of the kids below could be really obnoxious. "Rockcrawlers," they called those who lived in the higher reaches of the Rift; it was a jeering name for the Klytyk. "And speaking of fur-fruit, thanks for bringing us that basket. They may be the only things worth a trip below."

The net was as full now as Bili could safely carry. Jule tried not to be too obvious about getting rid of him, but he was anxious enough to get away from the weeds and deliver his repulsive burden. She managed to resist giving him advice about likely thermals and watched him soar off into space.

Finally she could let healer-training take over. Back in the cave she circled the hole, stopping when she was almost over the oozing wound. The Klytyk obviously knew she was there by her light and her movements; it tried a desperate lunge out of range but stopped with another shrill squeal of escaping air.

"I'm going to help," Jule called softly, hoping her tone would be reassuring. She didn't know how much understanding of human language they picked up in the mines.

She strapped the lightrod to her head and went to work, stripping the "eyes" from a leaf with her knife, pounding the gray-green mass with a loose rock until juice began to seep out. Then she held the pulp over the hole and squeezed until the thick sap dripped down right into the Klytyk's wound.

Even crushed the plant was sending a few root tendrils through her gloves; they'd have to be pulled out later with tweezers, but she felt no pain. That was the beauty of eye-weed. It not only cured infection, it provided instant anesthesia, and hardened in minutes into a flexible, protective "skin."

Jule went back for more leaves twice before the waves of pain diminished, leaving only a muted tremor of fear. What did it mean, she wondered, that the Klytyk's pain and fear came to her as clearly as any human's? It was a good thing the eye-weed didn't affect her like that when she crushed it. Everything did what was necessary for survival, but you had to draw a line somewhere.

In the case of the Klytyk, Jule realized suddenly, her own line had already been drawn, and it was not where the Council decreed.

There was more to be done if the creature was to have a chance at survival. Jule sat on the edge of the hole, measuring the distance. She was already taller than most earth-born humans; Marra said that the lower gravity made bones grow longer and lighter here. It would be no problem to lower herself onto the black shell below.

The problem would be in the reaction of her patient. Klytyk were never violent, even in self-defense; there would have been no chance of enslaving them otherwise. Their pointed beaks ("like the prow of a ship,"

24

Marra had once said, and then tried in vain to explain to Jule about ships and oceans full of water) extruded acid that could etch rock. Their great front claws could crush rock and hollow out caves, and the rows of rubbery appendages along their sides could cling to all but the steepest cliffs. Just the weight of an armored body could have pressed the life out of a fragile human.

It never had, but that might not mean much in the face of fear and desperation. Jule tried again to communicate, using a soft crooning tone as though reassuring a small child. "It's all right now, we'll make it all better, I'll touch you gently, gently . . ."

The fear retreated just a little. Jule poised on the rim of the gap, her canteen scraping against the rock. The sound gave her an idea. Klytyk were rarely observed to actually drink, but no sentient life on this world could fail to hold water sacred.

She poured a little of her precious allotment into her palm and tossed it toward the flare of black shell at the back of the huge head. Gleaming droplets rolled out of sight toward the hooded eyes and beak.

Then she dropped, sprawling, onto the hard wide back.

It lurched and heaved, of course, but only from the initial shock. Jule managed to stay on. When it stilled to a mere trembling she crawled toward the gaping wound, glancing at her surroundings as she went.

They were in a tunnel just big enough for a full-grown Klytyk. The one she straddled didn't quite fill it all; it must be as young, relatively speaking, as Jule herself. The marks of claws and etchings on the rock walls showed how the tunnel had been formed, or at least widened, but Jule had never heard of mines this high in the Rift; the Klytyk must use it for their own purposes. In this case, escape. But not without some help from her.

The wound was even worse than she had thought. Fragments of the metal implant were embedded in the flesh, and there were electrical burns around the original contact area.

The tools Jule carried in her belt pouch seemed absurdly small for something on this scale, but she had no choice. She'd have to work fast, too, before the numbing effect of the eye-weed wore off.

The larger bits of broken shell and metal could be pulled out by hand. It was when she had to lean close to the quivering flesh to use tweezers that the full strangeness of what she was doing hit her.

This huge creature, so far from human, or even mammal; what use were her anatomy lessons now? No inner bones, but rigid exoskeleton shielding the pale, vulnerable interior. A sudden wave of repulsion hit her, making her hands shake. How could she touch this alien monster?

Her head cleared, and her fingers moved again with their usual skill. The Klytyk were no aliens, and neither was she, in spite of her off-world ancestry. She had been born here. Her bones were formed from the elements of this world as much as any Klytyk's shell could be.

When she had done all she could in the uncertain

light and the Klytyk had begun to shift restlessly she dusted the wound with bright orange lichen powder. It had a regenerative effect on human tissue; it ought to work on Klytyk at least as well.

"Steady now, I'm going to stand up . . ." Whether it understood or not, the movement ceased long enough for her to get to her feet and jump to reach the rim of the hole. She pulled herself into the upper cave.

There were a few thick leaves left on the floor. Jule squeezed a little more sap into the cleaned wound, but it wasn't long before the black shell began to move and the Klytyk disappeared from view.

Jule felt a strange blend of elation and disappointment. Was that the end of it? Would she ever find out more about the creature she had helped?

She filled another net with eye-weed and shrugged back into her wing-harness. Harvesting the jewelmoss would take special tools and another trip. She might not do it right away; she didn't want Bili to connect the treasure with this particular cave.

Someone (or something) else had the same idea. When Jule soared past the spot she knew was right a few days later, there was no cave opening to be seen. The rockfall looked perfectly natural, but she didn't believe for a minute that the beak-shaped overhang had crumbled on its own. Couldn't they have trusted her?

Well, no, she supposed; they couldn't have taken that chance. She drifted lower along the cliff face, discouraged and dejected.

Five hundred feet below and to the east she found

that she hadn't been forgotten. First she saw the shape etched into the rock; it echoed her own spread-winged shadow, or the one she would have cast if the day had been clearer. Then, just in time, she saw the ledge below, barely wide enough to let her land.

There was no cave here, only a long, low niche, no deeper than the length of her arm, but when she reached in the shimmering glow of jewelmoss lit up the gray leather of her sleeve. There was more than she had ever heard of in one place. The clumps were already harvested, neatly carved out with just enough base rock left attached to keep them healthy. They could mean unimaginable riches . . . or they could provide resources to help in the struggle against slavery.

Jule took what she could carry and hid them closer to the home plateau in the little cave that had been her secret refuge since she was old enough to fly. It took several trips over the next few days to transport them all, and even then she wasn't ready to tell anyone, even Marra, all that had happened.

It would take time to sort out in her mind what she felt, what she could do. But she already understood that there was far more to being a healer than tending flesh and bone—and shell—and greater wounds than those of the body to be healed.

2064, OR THEREABOUTS

by David R. Bunch

He was just a tall spot moving slow out of the Down Provinces when first I picked him up on the Warn. But he came on dogged and inexorable until he stood dour and spent-seeming, frowning at my armored gates, the noon sun of a sun-flashing day glinting upon his sheathed face.

I allowed him through my gates one by one, when the weapons report and all the decontaminators signaled he was clean, and I saw that his heart was exposed as well as some of the gears activating the breath bags. There were tatters of flesh, and torn metal, over half of his upper shell. It was as though some giant claw, I thought, had ripped him across the chest in some accidental quick encounter. Or more it was, I thought, like a madman might work and rip at himself after some long time of frustration.

"You're hurt!" I impulsively said, a strange compassion working through me as I stared into his rusting sorrowing eyes.

"NO!" he said, putting down the small easel he carried, "not the way that you think I am hurt. The heart works well still, and the covering being off the gears of the chest does not slow them one whit. But I am hurt, deep-wounded, daily killed by the long unrewarded years of looking, not finding." He dropped his head forward then and his shoulders were bent, and I knew enough about burdens to know that he had one.

"Each of us seeks his own view of the Dream," he went on, "each in his limited way, each to his own degree of time-spent-in-searching looks for his Ultimate. Mine has been almost a total involvement, and the years seem growing late now, mine and the world's. That's why when you saw me, though perhaps I did not seem to be, I was speeding. I was almost to total maximum with my hinges and braces working, oh, I was on the trail of the Dream again, hotly. Coming down here."

"But why," I stammered, "why have you, an artist, come to this place of an obvious involvement in strength, a citadel of real firmness? I suppose you are en route?"

"NO!" He snapped his head up, the old shoulders straightened and the white metal strings in his beard trembled. His head shook on the spring-strips in his neck. "No, I am not en route, except in that larger sense that we are always en route as we wander here and look here. But I hope I am Here now, arrived. I hope I have found—after this to wander no more the Long Search."

"I—I don't understand." In my general uncertainty and surprise I trembled more than I meant to. Instinctively I looked to the better positioning of weapons men and edged a little nearer a steel sentry who stood nearby. "This is no artist's colony," I blurted, "nor an old painter's rest home. This is a working Stronghold, and we hold no dances for maimed Dream Seekers here. I would hope not to have to be unkind."

31

He ignored my words almost entirely. "Through the Dream Provinces," he continued, "word spread of a most wonderful armed place by the plastic lands of the steel dogs near the Valley of the Witch. A man was in a citadel there, according to rumors passed round, a New Processes man of a New Processes Land, re-placed, metal-shored, flesh-stripped to the very mini-mum of flesh allowable for mortal man. That man sat serenely living, month in and month out, years long, decades long, never influenced by family or friend or enemy, completing his great self through the days of his living, really living a Life. Surrounded by so many security devices and Walls and all the Wonderful Appliances of the Sciences that serve and nourish mankind in this year of Our Discoveries, 2064, he lounged like a superb nut, a giant seed in a giant shell, ripening day by day to new Meanings. After wander-ing life-long, frantically, the fear-tossed world and not finding—well, to see such beauteous calm—and Life-Meaning—I must before I die!

"Yes, I have been of the wanderers," he talked on, "the lost and searching wanderers, who sometimes never find because we pick, to look for, a Dream too shining to ever be." He plucked a small raveling piece of metal loose from his malleable nose. "Yes, they re-placed me, metal-alloyed me, gave me there at the last mostly a mechanical metallic heart, one perhaps as faultless and smooth-working as yours or your great master's. But I was never content to go behind some weapons and a Wall to live with the Wonderful

Appliances. In short, I could never quite find my place in the stability of the New Processes society. Something writhed unfed, always.

"Frantically it seems I was always chasing the wind to the edges of frightening bottomless caverns of Despair, while such as your great master, with what must have been a surer grasp of The Values, slipped with effortless beauteous calm into the chair of The Dream. I have longed to make some enduring monument; I have hungered after the Great Painting; ever haunted by questions I have tried throughout a long failure to express the Life-Meaning, the essence of YOU and ME. And now, changing my course a little, I have come to do it as a single portrait, one of your firm great master calmly in his chair! Right here in this Stronghold!"

More than a trifling alarmed now I looked at the gauntness of him where he stood trembling, his rusted metal flexing, sending up small squeaks and screams. And I noted how his flesh-strips with the years had gone all wrinkled and sere. There was a stench about him of old grease in the hinge joints, and certainly he needed an oil bath to brighten his metal shell.

What poor specimens profess to our greatest dreams and questions, I reflected. This smelly vagrant, I thought with the greatest contempt, peasant-robot-thing, probably didn't have a single Wall or weapons man to his name, and yet he staggers addle-waddle over the countryside, with his easel and paintbrushes, talking about his Ultimate, talking about Meaning. As though such as he had any right to question and conjecture! But when his rusting eyes with all their piercing sorrow looked into mine again, I felt a queer watery feeling, that was not fear, flood through my flesh-strips.

"Perhaps you have not had your introven," I said. "Perhaps you have food-hunger." I went for a needle and a cup of the special fluid that serves to nourish our flesh-strips, that small part of mortality the Rebuilders have had to leave between metal and metal, even here in Moderan.

When I came back he was lying along the floor, looking like the small beginnings of an interesting stack of scrap steel. His hands were over his face, the fingers spread, and except his eyes gleamed through his fingers like two brown fires, I would have thought him entirely "done with it all." With the snap of a rusty spring he came to a sitting position.

"I do not wish to dine," he said. "I am quite well and strong, really. It's just that so near to Dream's find, to trail's end, to final realization one grows a little fluttery in the dream bag, a little tight in the think box, oh God! oh God! A kind of tightening around the mind cups it is; a kind of great hammering of the heart that has waited so long comes on. And a throbbing beats just under the gears of the eyes to make one see phantom wings. One feels suddenly tired and close to death on the brink of the Great Jubilation. That's why I lay down."

He stood erect, just unfolded up from the floor with a snap of all his joints. In some ways it reminded me of an automatic tree coming out of the plastic earth-shell, the way they do when spring comes round to Big Calendar and someone thumbs the switch to Green Things in Season Control.

"Take me to him," he cried, "for it grows late, late in my years as well as old in the years of the world. Let us waste no more time. Take me to your great master, that man who sits living like a great firm nut, a splendid seed, the earth's finest fruit, ripening in the hulls of his Walls, guards, and guns. His Meaning I would record; such an adaptation, such a fearless calm in the face of the ever-lurking Disaster is surely the Beauty I have sought."

Unfortunately, at that juncture I had one of my panic times. Certain wheels had spun round, the slots had been spread, and in my mind now it was time for my cowardice. While he stood there waiting to be conducted to the Great Calm Face, I passed totally into the Trembly Country of Fear, my own personal Nation of Dread. While he stood watching, wondering, I went completely into my Cycle of Anguish, and I could not help how it was. I trembled violently; metal parts clanked and zinged; my face steel became so gaunt and distorted that metal-complaint started up a high shriek-and-whine. I started wildly to think of all the happenstance things that might befall me and my fort.

Though the sound-buzz was constant now, meaning that all was well in the Wonderful Appliances that often served me so well, how long would it be so? Let a wheel falter a thousand miles away, let a shaft break where a billion phantom buckets dropped uncountable billions of power droplets upon a blade, upon a thousand blades, and lights would blink, the wonderful buzz would go scratchy, and my fort would cough and catch its breath and flounder like a bent-down sick old man.

And the sun! what of of the sun? the giver of all. The sun burns up! The sun falls out of the sky! A bigger sun comes flying flaming out of the Great Yon and burps and my sun is wafted away, or even it eats my sun! opens up like some great boa mouth and gulps a small flaming egg.

Fears, Fears, FEARS! In my personal cycle, far in the Kingdom of Dread, I think of all the fears, fears founded, fears unfounded, fears old, fears new, fears not before dreamed up perhaps by any man—an attack! a space launch from far-off dangerous old Mars! Some strange metal-rot works all unknown, unsuspected, in my hinge joints for years! I fall into chaos and parts. Suddenly—What else is there but fears ever for any reasonable man? What? WHAT?

When I came back to a calmer place and found somehow the small firm Fortress of Hold in my groping mind, I saw how he waited and stared. A pounding as of hammers on huge steel tubes filled my metal ears then; wave on wave of shame washed up from my mortal strips. I clung to two steel men and braced my feet hard on a pillar of iron fitted around marble slabs.

Fighting hard I managed to meet the intensity of his gaze.

"There's no one here but me—I swear," I finally said, "I'm master here—I'm the one you would paint! Shall we move to my calmness chair?"

For a moment too intense to measure in the long hurling on of Time the brown balls of his eyes seemed awash in his battered head. His face steel wrinkled and screamed, the white threads of his beard trembled as if a sharp wind passed through. I watched the Dream finally die in the iron face of a man, and being what I was, there was no thing I could do.

"I'm sorry," I heard him say as from some immeasurably great distance, and I felt something of how sorry he really was for us all.

After a while he left, clutching his empty unused easel in a kind of greater desperation, it seemed—out through all the launchers and the Walls, the weapons tracking him, and seeing him go I felt I was watching a Dream at the very end of its road. He reeled toward the plastic valley of the steel dogs, and I went deeper into my complex to take me a calmness bath, and later I aimed to try with new nerve-strip rays to stay that trembling that had started up again all through my flesh-and-steel shell.

Later I heard how he was met at the edge of the Valley by a little masquerade new-metal dog carrying the barest of plastic bones marked THIS FOR THE MEANING SEEKER. Of course it was a wide joke sent up from the Palace of the Witch, and that was why the air over the

White Witch Valley was suddenly alive with big clown-faced balloons and the long guns of laugh salvoing out a full Ho-ho salute.

The masquerade dog, the gears and the punched cards in his head working perfectly, backed carefully away while the artist examined the bone. Handling it in other than the one prescribed way, of course, the artist caused the mined bone to explode, and his heart and colors and empty easel, as well as his metal shell and the few flesh-strips he owned, for a moment joined the Ho-ho salute and the big-balloon clown carnival high over White Witch Valley.

Considering his high seriousness, as well as the intensity of his try, it did seem, even to me, a most unsatisfactory way for him to go.

THE LOOKING GLASS

by Alethea Eason

A girl named Elena and an old woman named Marta lived on a lonely coast where the beaches were wild and the wind always blew. Their cottage rested behind a grove of eucalyptus trees. When Elena looked out her bedroom window at night, the trees resembled giants dancing madly, waving their hands at the stars. There was always a clutching at her heart as she watched. She feared that if one of the trees saw her face in the window she would be grabbed into its leafy arms, never to see Marta again.

One day, the two of them sat on a grassy knoll that rose in front of the cottage, sunning themselves, while Marta mended a hole in a fishing net. Elena watched Marta work and thought how the trees looked almost human as they danced at night. Then, for the first time, she wondered if Marta and she were really all alone.

"Are there any other people besides you and me?"

Marta didn't look up. "Not in this world."

"Then how did we get here?" Elena asked. Her nose itched and when she scratched it, she left a smudge of dirt at its tip. Her face was freckled from spending most of her days out of doors. The sun had bleached her hair to a sandy white.

"We were sent," Marta said.

"By whom?"

Marta's hair was the same shade as the child's. She

had lines in her face, especially when she smiled, but Elena was thankful she was not very old, not yet.

"All of them. They all wanted us here. I found you one morning, sitting as calmly as you please, right here in this spot of grass."

Elena frowned as Marta continued working. "Were we bad?"

"Heavens, no. We are here for good reasons. There's much we have to do. The work is mine now, but someday it will be yours." Marta yanked on the net and was satisfied her mending would hold. She stood up before the child could ask more questions and gathered the net in her arms. "The tide is low. Go to the rocks, and bring back a pail of mussels for dinner. When you return, I'll have a surprise."

When her bucket was full, Elena looked out at the sea. The surface of the water was eye level, and the sea seemed to breathe as it rose and sank. She climbed out of the low-lying pools so she could see the horizon, stood for a while studying the water, and wondered what was on the other side.

Something told her that she stood at the end of the world, and she felt fear. More than anything, she wanted to be inside the cottage, safe with Marta, the warmth of a cooking fire soothing away the queasiness filling her stomach. She picked up the bucket and hurried as fast as she could over the rocks to home.

"Where is the surprise?" Elena asked as soon as she ran into the cottage. She wanted to tell Marta of the fear she had felt, but couldn't find the words to describe it.

Marta took a frying pan from its hook and poured wine from a large green bottle into it.

"In a little while. Elena, do you ever wonder where we get the things we need? This pan, for example, the wine we cook with, or even this bottle that holds the wine?"

Elena shook her head. The things they needed had always been with them.

Marta said no more until dinner was over. Elena's uneasiness grew. She was told to clear the table and then to wipe it clean. As she worked, Marta went into her room. When she came out, she held an object Elena had never seen before and laid it facedown on the table.

"I use this to create all we need," Marta explained. "I made the sea, the trees, and the birds that fly above us. I even made the frying pan because it was needed. I could have created another world, but I have memories of the sea, and so here we are."

"But how did we get here?"

"Somewhere deeper than their deepest dreams, the people in the old world made this place. They made you, and they made me. We are here to remember them, to bring them to this world someday."

Elena pointed to the object on the table. "What is that?"

"A looking glass," Marta said. "It's like a window, of sorts, but you must promise me to never look into it until after my death. The power it holds will be yours, but only then."

"What do you do with it?"

"The glass helps me to see. While you sleep, I remake the world each night, but you are to be the one who will

finally make this world big enough to hold the others."
A troubled look passed over Elena's face, so Marta
added, "But that won't happen for a long, long time."

Elena wanted to grip the whorled handle and finger
the inlay of abalone that decorated its back. At the same
time, she was afraid of it.

"Does the pattern make a sun or a star?" she asked.

"Both, for light is the source of all things."

"My head hurts," Elena said. "I can't fit your words into it."

Marta leaned over and kissed her. "There's no need it
has to. But listen to me: a part of your readiness, the test of
your power, will be to resist the glass. Do you understand?"

Elena yawned. "No."

"Even still, when I am away, out of the house, you
are not to touch it."

"I won't. I promise," Elena said. But something told
her that the promise would be hard to keep. "May I go
to bed now?"

As Elena was being tucked into bed, she said, "I wish
you made the eucalyptus trees less scary."

"I didn't know they bothered you. They are another
memory I seem to have. Their leaves would be used
when people caught colds."

"What are colds?"

"Something I chose not to bring into this world."

Elena woke in the middle of the night with the same fear that
had claimed her at the beach. She got out of bed and walked
to Marta's room. Marta was sitting in her rocking chair, her
back toward the door, holding the mirror before her face.

Elena watched the back of the chair, afraid to lift her eyes. She didn't want to create the world, night after night, not now, not ever. Her feet were cold, but she couldn't move until Marta put the glass in her lap and turned to look at her.

"Come here."

Elena walked to the chair. "I don't want to do it, Marta. How can you think of everything in the world each night?"

"I've been here for what would be lifetimes at home. And once something has been created and put in its place—the sea, for instance—all it needs is a little attention."

"Don't you ever sleep?"

"I no longer need to. Put your slippers on and come with me."

Marta led Elena to the back of the cottage where the eucalyptus waved gently in the wind.

"I don't want you to make the same mistake as I did," Marta said.

"What was that?"

"I didn't trust myself." They walked under the shaggy branches of the trees, through the bark that lay in piles on the ground. Marta picked up a leaf and broke it in half. "Smell this."

Elena took a whiff. "It smells musty."

"And underneath that?"

"Something strong."

"And healing. I don't want you to be afraid of anything you don't understand."

*   *   *

44

Marta hung the looking glass on a peg on the wall near the cooking fire. Elena thought about the glass every day, wanting to peer into it to see what would be there. Sometimes, when Marta was away, she would stand before the glass and study the pattern of the star, thinking about what she would bring into the world.

"I would create someone to play with," she whispered to it one day.

The star began to glow slightly. Elena rubbed her eyes, but when she opened them again, the light was still there.

"Can you hear me?"

The star shone even brighter.

"I would like there to be someone to talk to who's my own age. Could you do that?"

The light began to pulse.

"And I would want more sweet things to eat. And some sort of soft animal that wasn't wild that could be mine."

Look into my face, Elena.

Elena stepped back.

Turn me over.

"I can't do that."

Of course you can.

The voice was hypnotic.

Touch me.

Elena reached up. Her fingertips brushed the handle. A searing pain shot across them, burning her as though she had touched the stove. She pulled her hand back and put her fingers in her mouth.

The next time won't hurt. I promise. That's the worst of it. Turn me over and you can have anything you want.

45

Elena covered her ears and ran out of the house and down to the sea. The pounding surf quieted her heart, but then she lifted her eyes to the horizon.

"I don't want to be alone!" she cried out, sensing the emptiness beyond her. She wanted to go back to the house and do the bidding of the looking glass, but she made herself stay on the beach until she knew Marta would be home.

When she walked into the cottage, Marta was scrubbing dirt from some wild carrots she had found.

"I forgot all about these," Marta said.

Elena wanted Marta to know what she had done. She wanted to be warned again, *Do not touch the looking glass*. But the old woman hummed a tune to herself and continued scrubbing.

"Why don't you keep the looking glass in your room anymore?"

Marta straightened and turned around. The way she looked at Elena told the girl that she knew more than Elena had assumed.

"I can't do that," Marta replied. "The greater it compels you, the more you hold back, the stronger your power will be."

"I don't want anything to do with this!" Elena shouted and ran into her room, slamming the door.

Elena refused to be alone with the glass after that. Whenever Marta went out, she followed her. She was grateful Marta said nothing.

One spring morning she went for a walk by herself.

The grass was green, and the toes of her shoes became wet from the dew. She walked farther than she had ever gone before. There were more trees now, their branches budding with flowers and slips of light green leaves. A rabbit scurried from a hedge, and Elena decided to follow it through a jumble of rocks that loomed ahead of them.

When the rabbit disappeared from sight, Elena climbed the rocks. She sat down and dangled her feet over the edge, but then pulled them up suddenly, hugging herself.

There was nothing below her.

Now she knew she had seen the whole world, from the rocks to the sea's horizon. Beyond these places was a void, a place where nothing had ever been.

She tried to think about what it would be like not to exist, to step into the nothing below her. Beads of sweat gathered on her forehead.

"If I fell down there, I would disappear. I would be nothing."

The thought overwhelmed her, and she stood up and ran home.

Marta was not there. Elena threw herself on the bed. Through the doorway, she heard the looking glass call her name.

Elena, one glimpse and you will no longer be afraid.

She pulled a pillow over her head.

You would understand everything.

The pull of the glass was strong. Elena climbed out of bed. Her body shook as she walked toward it. The only thing she wanted now was not to be scared anymore. She gazed at the star. It glowed softly, and she lifted her hand.

Marta walked through the door. Elena jerked her hand back and stood guiltily before the glass.

"Did you touch it?"

Elena could not answer.

"Did you touch it?" Marta's voice grew anxious.

"No," Elena answered. *Not this time*, she thought. "But I wanted to."

And then words tumbled out as she told Marta what had happened at the rocks, how afraid she was of becoming a part of the nothingness, how she had touched the handle once and her fingers burned for days.

"You *must* resist the glass." Marta took a deep breath and then let it go. "You have resisted, or you would have looked into it long before now."

Elena put her head on Marta's shoulder, worried that she would not be able to help herself, that someday the glass would finally compel her to look into its face.

The next morning, Marta picked a basket of strawberries for breakfast. Elena prepared them while Marta had her first cup of tea.

"There must be *something* on the other side of the rocks," Elena said as she worked.

"No, dear. There isn't anything there."

Elena carried the strawberries to the table, along with a pitcher of cream. "But how can nothing exist? How can we be alive in the middle of nothing?"

Marta scooped the strawberries into her bowl and poured the thick cream over them. Elena sat down and watched her eat. Marta closed her eyes, savoring the taste. When she opened them, she looked at Elena.

"The world that sent us was dying. There have been others like us sent here to create a new home, but none have been able." Marta shook her head. "All of us have failed. When things have seemed hopeless, before the time the glass rightfully belonged to us, we've all looked into it. Elena, you are the last one of us. You must be strong."

"I'm sure I have no talent for making things."

"You may have the greatest gift of all precisely because they didn't send their memories with you. You can create a new world without being burdened by the old one."

After that day, Marta would sit with Elena on the beach and explain how she would look into the glass and think about all that was around them—how the gulls and crabs, the eucalyptus and cedars, the rains that kept their cistern filled would appear and then become real in their world. Marta, from time to time, would make something new: another mile of coastline, a family of raccoons, or a brilliant patch of poppies.

The years passed, and Elena grew into a young woman.

"You talk and talk," she complained one day after Marta pointed to a spout of water blowing from a whale's back, one of her recent creations. "But how am I to know what to make?"

It was a familiar complaint. Marta's answer was the same as always: "When the time comes, you will know. The pictures will come, and you will create a world that should have been, but never was."

Marta's words often reassured Elena—for a little while, at least—but today she was filled with doubt.

Marta stood up slowly. She walked back to the cottage, using her walking stick with every step. Elena watched the bank of fog that had been resting on the water all afternoon slowly make its way inland. She stayed until the sun disappeared, and only then did she walk home.

The next morning, Marta could not get out of bed. She took Elena's hand and said, "Go outside and tell me what you see."

"I don't want to leave you."

"You must go now," Marta insisted, so Elena ran out of the house and down the path to the beach. The fog was thick, and she could not see the ocean, nor hear the pounding of the surf.

The sun came out behind the fog bank. She stepped back.

There was nothing before her—no swells of water, no gulls singing in the air. There was no longer the smell of salt in the wind. The sea had vanished.

She rushed back to the cabin. The trees on the hills surrounding the cottage were being erased, then the hills themselves disappeared. The sky was vanishing and only a small patch of blue hovered overhead.

"What is happening?" Elena asked as she ran to Marta's room.

Marta's eyes were closed. Light disappeared from the window. Nothing was left in her world but the cottage and silence.

The silence was worse than the fear Elena had felt as a little girl looking at the horizon, worse than her panic at the rocks. She didn't know if she would be trapped in the house forever or if, in the next breath, the silence would engulf the room and both Marta and she would become part of the darkness.

The looking glass beckoned.

I am the only hope you have.

There was a candle on the bed stand. Elena lit it and walked to the glass. She took it from the wall, expecting her hand to be seared. But the handle was only warm, the last warmth left in the room. Sitting down on Marta's bed, she stared at the pattern on its back. The star glowed brightly.

Look into me and turn back time. Marta does not have to die. Look into me and make it so.

Elena wanted nothing more than to have things the way they used to be and for Marta to be well again. Squeezing her eyes shut, she turned the glass over. As she was about to open them, she heard Marta's voice as it was long ago.

You must resist the looking glass.

Elena turned her face away and pointed the glass toward Marta. She barely breathed, knowing if she moved she would be lost. The glass became heavier and her body ached. She was about to drop it when she heard Marta say, "Look at me."

She didn't move, afraid the glass was playing another trick.

"Look at me, dear."

Elena could no longer resist. She opened her eyes. Marta peered into the glass, her face at peace, and when she looked at Elena for the last time, her eyes held a light that seemed to come from the stars.

The next morning, Elena took the looking glass to the beach. The sun was warm and lit her skin, striking it like a match. She had remade the sea, not really knowing how. She walked to the water. The waves splashed gently over her feet.

"What would have happened if I had looked into you before Marta died?" she asked the looking glass.

She turned it over and saw herself sitting by Marta's side. The bed was a raft in the darkness. The cottage had vanished.

One moment Elena held Marta's hand; the next, Marta was gone. The darkness then streamed from their world, swallowing suns flung far out in space. Elena watched other worlds disappear and galaxies collapse upon themselves.

You were the last hope, the looking glass whispered. Then everything was silent.

Elena fell to the sand. She wrapped her arms around her body to stop shaking and watched the waves to calm the pounding of her heart.

After a long while, she sighed. "I have a world to create."

But first there was the most difficult task. She carried Marta's body, so light now, to the beach and made a bed of driftwood and dried bark from the eucalyptus trees. She then held the glass so that it caught the rays of the sun. The wood smoldered, then the flames soared.

Elena knew someone was looking into another glass, remembering Marta. There was no longer emptiness beyond the horizon. Another world was evolving where possibilities could be pulled like bright fish from the sea.

FREE WILL

by John C. Bunnell

But what does it do?" I asked Dr. Forrester, eyeing the weird-looking device in the center of his laboratory.

Before he answered, he pulled a detector from the pocket of his lab coat and waved it around the room. "We're clean," he said after studying its readout. "All right, Petra, I guess it's safe to tell you. This is a reality-separation generator, and we're going to save the universe with it."

I took another look at the "reality-separation generator." It looked like a cross between a fish tank, a video arcade game, and a model of a space telescope. Which made sense, considering that we'd assembled it from a fish tank, nine different computers, three VCRs, a laser-disc player, a box of aluminum foil, and an electric radio-controlled model hovercraft. Dr. Will Forrester might be one of the most brilliant scientists in St. Woodlawn, but he didn't have much money for parts.

"Save the universe?" I said. "I thought that's what the Shogun Scouts were for."

Dr. Forrester shook his head. "That's just it," he said. "The Shogun Scouts are the only reason this universe exists in the first place. We were created—invented out of whole cloth—by people in another universe, the same way writers in Hollywood create Saturday morning cartoons. In a sense, we *are* a Saturday morning cartoon, or at least we're living on the inside of one."

"We?" I echoed, looking at him. The Shogun Scouts were teenagers, or so the newspapers said. Dr. Forrester was young for a Ph.D. in theoretical physics—maybe twenty-five—but too old for him to be one of the five super-warriors who guarded St. Woodlawn from the Black Tong.

"I'm sorry, Petra," he said. "It was too dangerous to tell you before. I was one of the original Shogun Scouts—Emerald, to be precise. Jen-Dee recruited me when I was fourteen, maybe two years older than you are now."

I sucked in a startled breath. Jen-Dee was said to be a nearly immortal being who had created the Shogun Jewels dozens of centuries ago, and advised the Shogun Scouts in their ongoing battle with the Black Tong and its leader, who was known only as Master Obsidian. At least that was the popular opinion. Most of what people knew about the Scouts came from cheap tabloid newspapers and cheesy investigative TV shows. There'd been a couple of books written about them, but it was hard for readers to tell what was true and what the authors had made up for lack of reliable data.

"Original?" I said, my voice quavering. "But how? There've been Shogun Scouts in St. Woodlawn since before the Civil War. Remember last year, when they found a Scout insignia in the time capsule buried when City Hall was built?"

He laughed, but not out of amusement. "That insignia belonged to me once," he said. "Trust me, I was one of the first Scouts. We used to go back in time every so often, though never intentionally. That was when I started to suspect something was wrong with the universe—we'd keep running into ancestors who looked just like us, right down to the birthmarks. The odds against copies of the same five people showing up all over history are so astronomical you'd need half the paper on Earth to write all the zeroes in the number."

It was a wild story, but it made a weird kind of sense. The news reports all agreed that the Shogun Scouts had lost and replaced members of their team over the eight years since their activities had first become public. Just how much turnover there'd been was uncertain, but everyone knew that of the five original Shogun Jewels, only three—Diamond, Ruby, and Topaz—remained. Emerald had been destroyed and replaced by Jade, and the Black Tong had transmuted Sapphire into Onyx, forcing the Scouts to create Tourmaline.

As for Dr. Forrester having been Emerald, that was possible, too. He was the right age. Popular wisdom said that Emerald had indeed been a scientific genius (as was the current Ruby). And a "reality-separation generator" was about as plausible as most of the other techno-toys that the Scouts and the Black Tong tended to leave in their wake. The regular scientific community regarded most of these as flat-out impossible, and generally couldn't explain how they worked—but you could still see the twelve-foot stuffed rat in the city museum and the roughly human-shaped patch of dead ground in Cardinal Park where a Black Tong exterminator had literally disintegrated last year. And even after four years of trying, no one at the Metatech plastics factory could tell what the Scout helmet they'd acquired—left in the street after an unusually messy confrontation with Tong ninjas—was made of.

"Okay," I said cautiously. "So you used to be Emerald. How does that prove the universe is in trouble, and how is that thing going to fix it?"

"It's a matter of free will," said Dr. Forrester. "Have you ever wondered why no one's ever managed to actually kill Master Obsidian, or how the Scouts always manage to survive the Tong's attacks?"

"Well . . ." I said, ". . . I guess it's always seemed like they were a pretty even match."

"And yet," Dr. Forrester insisted, "not once in eight years has one of the Tong's takeover or mass destruction plots actually worked. Sure, they knock down a few buildings every couple of weeks. But every single time Master Obsidian tries to poison the water supply, or blow up City Hall, or hypnotize the entire population, *nothing ever happens*. Yet he always gets away, he always has a new plan ready to go a week or two later, and none of the nine hundred or so ninjas the police have nailed has ever been able to tell them where to find the Tong's base. Do you realize how statistically improbable that is?"

I didn't try to work out the numbers, but when he put it that way, it did seem strange. Master Obsidian's failure rate made him look unbelievably inept, but his talent for escapes and his endless supply of minions and ideas made him look unbelievably competent. "I'll take your word for it," I said. "But what about free will?"

Dr. Forrester smiled thinly. "The only way a situation like that of the Scouts and the Tong could go on as long as it has," he said, "is for it to have been engineered. It's an artificial construct. And since the tools the adversaries use don't follow the normal scientific principles of this universe, it follows that whoever engineered the conflict is from somewhere else."

I turned the idea over in my mind. "Well, maybe. Couldn't it be super-powerful aliens from this universe? Time travelers from the future? God?"

"No, no, and for all practical purposes, yes. Aliens or time travelers couldn't control all the variables. But yes, the forces that created the Shogun Scouts are, essentially, stand-ins for God. And that's why we have to stop them."

"Good grief," I said, swallowing hard. "Did you hear what you just said? If you're going up against God, aren't you guaranteed to lose by definition?"

"That," said Dr. Forrester, "is why this lab is in a rented garage instead of on a university campus. It's why I recruited you as my assistant instead of hiring a graduate student. And it's why we've built this generator from odds and ends instead of buying or special-ordering the specific parts I needed." He tapped the device once, then rubbed his hands together in satisfaction.

I eyed the generator skeptically. "I don't think I get it."

Dr. Forrester sighed. "You have to understand that I didn't leave the Scouts on purpose. Jen-Dee more or less arranged for me to be kicked out, and at the time I had no idea why." This was disturbing news. Jen-Dee was supposed to be one of the white hats. If he had deliberately dismissed one of his own Shogun Scouts, there was more going on than met the eye.

"What I realized later," he went on, "was that I was getting too old and too experienced to maintain the balance of power. If I'd stayed with the Scouts much longer, I think we might actually have taken out Master Obsidian. If we'd been allowed to, that is—in a couple of the last battles I was in, I felt as if I wasn't fighting at full strength. Now I don't think I was. I think the Jewel was limiting the power of my attacks, preventing me from inflicting permanent damage."

"Whooo," I breathed softly. "That's weird. And if you're right, it would explain why most of the other Scouts have been sidelined over time."

"Exactly," said Dr. Forrester. "And most of them have never been the same since. As Scouts, they had extraordinary lives—once that stopped, so did most of their ability to excel. And nobody *except* the Scouts ever seems to truly accomplish any lasting good. Think about it. Have you ever read about a scientific breakthrough the Scouts didn't get involved with? A peace agreement signed with a foreign country? A space mission the Black Tong didn't try to disrupt? Can you tell me what movies won Oscars last year? What books won Pulitzer Prizes? Who was elected President? What country St. Woodlawn is in?"

"Well . . ." Abruptly, I realized that I couldn't answer a single one of Dr. Forrester's questions. I shook my head at him, not trusting myself to speak.

"So you see it," he said. "That's why we're doing this. Luckily for us, whoever developed this universe left a loophole. Nearly all the other Scouts got all their abilities purely from the Shogun Jewels, but not me. I could handle the weird science Jen-Dee and the Tong use in or out of uniform. And that didn't stop after Jen-Dee fired me. I'm *still* a techno-wizard, but it's limited to the kind of gonzo gadgetry I was building before."

I looked at the reality-separation generator thoughtfully. "I think I see. If this really is someone's Saturday morning cartoon, then it's a formula plot. So if your character was defined as 'can invent whatever gizmo is needed to resolve a given situation,' that rule still holds. And if you invent something that's designed to split our whole universe off from the guys writing the cartoon, it'll probably do just that—as long as you can keep them from noticing until it's too late to stop you."

Dr. Forrester really smiled for the first time since I'd met him. "That's it exactly. And now the device is ready to activate."

"And once it's been activated," I said in a low, awed voice, "everyone's destiny will be their own. People will be able to break out of the formula. Someone who used to be an 'extra' won't be stuck as an extra for the rest of her life. And the Scouts will be free to pound Master Obsidian into glass-dust once and for all."

"You *do* understand," Dr. Forrester breathed. "I knew I could rely on you."

"Thank you!" I told him. "That means a lot."

"Well, then," he said, "let's do it. Hand me the remote, would you please?"

I picked up the generator's remote control, and returned his smile. "I don't think so," I said. "It was a brilliant idea, but I can't let you carry it out."

Dr. Forrester's face turned solid white. "Wh-what? No!" He jumped toward me, reaching for the object in my hand.

I ran a finger over a control on the underside of the ring on my right hand. "Yes," I said, as crimson light shimmered around me and the Shogun Ruby blazed to life.

With a casual gesture, I squeezed the generator's remote control into a wad of plastic roughly the size of a pizza-pocket and dropped it to the floor. Then I lifted my ring hand and pointed it at the generator itself. A bolt of flickering red energy shot across the room and struck the device, which flashed through all the colors of the rainbow in the space of two or three seconds, then imploded with a surprisingly soft *bang*. All that remained after the discharge was a small mound of rubble.

All the energy went out of Dr. Forrester, who simply stared at the remains of his invention in shock. "But why?" he asked hollowly. "The Scouts are supposed to uphold justice. Why leave this world locked into an endless loop?"

"Justice cuts both ways," I said. "You made two critical mistakes. The Scouts' one unbreakable rule isn't upholding justice—it's following Jen-Dee's instructions. And Jen-Dee's defining characteristic is that he knows anything and everything the Scouts need to learn in order to preserve order."

"So he knew all along." The former Emerald's voice was barely audible.

I nodded. "Of course. And he arranged for me to be available when you went hunting for a trustworthy lab assistant. I've only been Ruby for three months; there was virtually no chance you'd identify me."

"It fits." Dr. Forrester sighed. "But it still doesn't explain why. Don't you want free will?"

"We can't afford it," I told him. "You explained it yourself: we Scouts have been rotated off the team after we develop a certain amount of experience. But Master Obsidian has been there from the beginning, and by now has more combat experience than all the current Scouts put together. If we take the gloves off now, the odds are that he'll take us out. And then nobody will ever win an Oscar, or a Pulitzer, or cure cancer, or go to Mars."

He stared at me, eyes wide. "Maybe. But maybe not. Maybe you'd find the strength to beat him, or Jen-Dee would."

"We can't take the risk."

"Then you might as well kill me now," Dr. Forrester said. "I'll keep trying, you know. I can't give up, even if it means taking on the Scouts."

I shook my head. "You know I can't do that," I said. "The Scouts don't kill, not deliberately. Besides, now you're part of the balance you were talking about. You're right, you will keep trying—it's in your nature. But we'll always be there to stop you at the last moment. We'll have to be." A thought struck me, and I let out a short laugh. "Look on the bright side. At least you've managed to broaden the formula. Now the Scouts have two arch-villains to battle instead of one."

When I left, he was sitting on the floor in front of the smashed generator, eyes closed, tears running down his face.

But I knew it wouldn't last. He'd recover. And the Shogun Scouts would be ready when he did.

It was our job, after all.

EGG SHELLS

by Nina Kiriki Hoffman

Fern smoothed out her old shell, laid it on the bed, and patted it flat. Almost transparent, it looked faintly grayish pink, and it was as soft to the touch as camellia petals—faintly soapy.

She opened the room's in-chute and picked up the next shell. It glowed pale caramel and tingled with life.

For a moment she stared at her unshelled self in the mirror: awkward in the elbows and knees, so thin her bones showed white through her pale skin; eyes a rain-washed gray; buzz-cut hair a tarnished metal brown.

Fern had lived looking like that from the time she was born until she turned ten, and had started shelling three years ago. She hated her base look.

Old holo-images of her mother looked like that— pale, thin, and bony. Her mother had been born too long ago to test-shell the way Fern and everyone she knew in school did. But Mom had picked a shell and changed after Fern was born. Mom had brown skin, white-blonde hair, and jewel-green eyes now.

Fern opened the slit down the new shell's back and slid inside it. She stroked its surface until it attached to her own skin, then stood with her eyes closed while this shell changed her into someone else. When it was done, she opened her eyes.

Oh, yes. Much better. Her body had filled out and

grown muscular. She checked the mirror again. She looked strong. She lifted her chin and smiled at herself. Her skin had darkened to a coffee-with-cream shade, and her eyes had turned gold. Short, fuzzy, black hair capped her head. She touched it with newly dark fingers, liking the feel of its tight curls. The sensitivity in these fingers pleased her, too.

She took a shower to get the new shell firmly settled. Water pounded it onto her, stapling it down.

While she showered she got to know herself. Smooth, dark skin with muscles just under the surface, a little boyish, pale palms and soles of the feet. Strange but good.

By the time she dried off, the old shell had dissolved into powder on the bed. She wished they wouldn't do that. She always forgot it was going to happen, and it made a mess. She stripped the bed and threw the pink-powdered sheets into the laundry chute.

"Fern?" Mother called from outside her door.

"Just a minute." Her new voice sounded warm and rich. She went to the in-chute and found a yellow dress, tossed it on over her head. It slid down and fitted perfectly. The clothes that showed up with new shells usually did. A small yellow pouch lay in the in-chute. Fern picked it up.

She put on underwear, but decided to skip socks.

"Fern? You're going to be late for the bus."

Fern slipped flat black shoes on, grabbed her carry-pouch, dropped the yellow case into it, and dashed to the door.

"Oh!" said Mother.

Fern ran her hand over her short hair, ventured a smile.

Mother touched her cheek. "Lovely," she said in a faint voice.

Fern picked up her datacase by the front door. Its cover had shifted to yellow to match her dress. She slipped it into her carrypouch, too.

The hoverbus was a little late. Just as well.

Sarah had saved her the same seat as always. Fern sat down, smoothing her skirt beneath her.

Sarah's new shell had big breasts and a perpetually half-open mouth, with vivid red lips and small, even teeth. Her new hair was long, curly, and blond, and her new eyes were toffee-brown. She looked surprised.

Fern had worn a shell sort of like that a few shifts ago, and she had hated it.

Flipping her eyelashes, Sarah smiled. "Three boys tried to sit by me." She shrugged. "First time that's happened."

"What would happen if we didn't sit in the same place all the time?"

"*Eww*," said Sarah. "Don't. I wouldn't know you."

Fern peered into her carrypouch. She took out the yellow accessories pouch and tapped it open. A golden charm bracelet and small gold star earrings dropped out.

"That would be weird," Fern said, fastening the bracelet around her left wrist. "But it might be interesting." She slipped the stars into holes in her ears.

"Puh-leeeeeze," Sarah said. "Don't go there. How would we get through the day?"

Fern quietly gazed at Sarah. Would they *really* not know each other? They had been best friends since kindergarten. No matter what shell Sarah wore, she always twisted her hair when she was puzzled or frustrated, and she sucked her bottom lip into her mouth when she was thinking hard. Sarah might be able to hide for a little while, but Fern was sure she'd figure out who Sarah was, given time.

She wasn't sure Sarah would know her back, though. Did Fern have habits that Sarah knew? Things she didn't even know she did?

Fern looked at all the strangers on the bus. People she'd been going to school with for ages, but she didn't know who they were just yet, except for the ones who sat in the same seats all the time. Some people switched around a lot, especially the ones who didn't have friends. With new shells, they might be able to pretend to be interesting. Maybe they could fool somebody . . . until roll call in first class, anyway.

When she had started shelling three years ago, Fern had been totally confused every time everyone got new shells. She could memorize names and faces much faster now.

Sometimes people wore the same shells as long as a month. Sometimes they changed after two days. Most of the time, they spent a couple of weeks in each shell. Fern didn't know she was going to change until she checked the alert light on the in-chute when she woke up each morning. If it was lit, there was a new shell to test.

Usually, everybody changed shells on the same day. Once, about five of the boys had stayed in the same shells for an extra couple of weeks, and Fern had felt strange and confused. She couldn't get herself to talk to them.

Fern took out her datacase and opened her shell journal. She made a few notes about what this shell looked like and how it felt. Then she jumped to the top of the file and peeked at her description of her first shell.

Whoa. It seemed like ages ago, but it was only three years. How many shells had she had? She scrolled down through the file. Some of them she couldn't even remember.

A boy two seats ahead of her turned and held up a small card with the name "Mica" on it. If he was actually Mica, he was shorter than he had been yesterday, and much thinner. He had long red hair and pale gray eyes.

Maybe it was someone else holding up a card with Mica's name on it. Fern frowned. The boy was sitting in Mica's seat. She might as well act as if he were Mica. She flickered two fingers at him, and he smiled.

Sarah nudged her. "Did you do the homework?"

Fern switched programs in her datacase. She couldn't remember doing her homework, but she always felt confused after changing shells. She tapped subject folders. Answer sheets scrolled down the screen, most of them filled out. Look at all the history, math, and science she had known yesterday! Or maybe she had just had a smart shell.

She slowed the scroll and stared at an equation for a little while, until her mind clicked and it made sense again. Some things left with the shells, and some things stayed with her.

"Let me see," Sarah said, reaching for the datacase.

Fern yawned and handed Sarah her answers. She flexed her arms, made muscles. They felt wonderful, sleek and powerful. Gym class would be so easy in this shell. Maybe Ms. Bark would say something nice.

Ms. Bark never seemed to follow anybody's transition from one shell to another. She was continually confused about who was who. "Count off," she'd say. "Okay! Number One, you're the pitcher. Number Three, you're the catcher . . ."

Nobody got good grades in her class.

Sarah said Ms. Bark was one of those people who believed shelling was evil and refused to cooperate with it. Fern thought maybe Ms. Bark was too lazy to figure out who people were. But every once in a while, she said something nice to an athletic shell.

Finally, Fern had one.

"Are you sure about this one?" Sarah asked, pointing to an essay answer to a history question.

"Don't copy that," Fern said. "You can't have exactly the same answer as I do to an essay question, stupid. They'll know one of us is copying."

"I was going to put it in my own words, but it sounds wrong."

Fern glanced at the original question: Why was the practice of shelling instituted?

What a dumb question.

"When student uniformity could not be enforced through dress codes and when shelling technology became available, it was thought . . ." Fern frowned. Dumb question, dumber answer.

For a second, she imagined an unshelled life. Stuck forever with that ugly wraith of a body.

At sixteen, they would choose permanent shells. But they didn't have to choose the shells they were born with.

And if you paid a lot of money, you could switch again later on.

"This doesn't make sense," Sarah said. "If they want us to all be the same, how come we're all different all the time?"

"I think it was, like, they thought if we knew what it felt like to be a bunch of different people, we'd understand that we're all the same inside," Fern said, tensing and untensing her legs just because it felt so good and she liked watching the muscles ripple and release beneath the smooth, dark skin. She shrugged. "I don't get it. It didn't make sense in the textfile, either."

"So, you're just saying it back?"

"Uh-huh." Their teachers didn't like them to parrot textfiles. But it was good enough for a C, and sometimes Fern just didn't care about the material.

"I'll make something up," Sarah said. She tapped her keyboard.

One of the boys behind them leaned forward and stared at Sarah's new breasts. He licked his lips.

"Eww!" cried Sarah, shrinking away from him.

"Yum," he said. He widened his eyes.

"Cut it out, Cody," Fern said, shoving the boy's head back.

"I'm not Cody," he said. He was dark-haired and

freckle-splattered, with narrow blue eyes and lots of large teeth.

"Sure you are. This wasn't funny last time, either."

"I'm not Cody," he repeated.

Fern stared at him, trying to figure out if he was kidding. She glanced at everybody in the bus and, for a dizzying moment, all their faces meshed and melted and swam and reformed, until she thought she didn't know anyone. What if she got on the wrong bus one day and couldn't even tell?

What if Sarah wasn't Sarah?

Fern sat and let the possibilities shudder through her. It was scary. Was everybody actually the same inside? Didn't your shell shape you? Sometimes she knew things in one shell she forgot in another. And for sure the boys had been a lot different to her when she had had big breasts. Once she had had a fat shell, and that had been different, too. People looked away from her. Some teachers ignored her, even when her desk answer light was lit.

Today she felt strong and beautiful. Yesterday she had been in a really normal shell, and everything had been ordinary.

Lots of people chose ordinary shells for their ultimate shells. Why?

"Hey, lady," said the not-Cody boy, still staring at Sarah's chest. "I want some of that."

Maybe he really wasn't Cody. Cody had never said anything so gross.

Or maybe his shell was making him act different?

Maybe boy shells did that. Boys always got boy shells,

and girls always got girl shells. Somebody said they were working on cross-gender shells, but it was a much more complicated technology and would take a while to develop. Fern imagined her own children switching sexes and looks every couple of weeks.

How would you know to love them? What if the children came home to the wrong house one day? What if no one could tell?

Fern glared at the freckle-faced boy. "It doesn't matter who you are," she said. "Just quit it!" She pushed him again. His eyes got slittier, but he sat back.

Fern glanced at Sarah, who sniffled a little bit. So she didn't like that kind of attention, either. Another shock of dislocation shuddered through Fern as she wondered whether this actually *was* Sarah.

Whoever she is, she thinks she's my best friend, Fern thought. She sniffed the back of her hand. It smelled alien—cinnamon and strange.

She hesitated, then set her hand on the seat cushion between her and Sarah.

Sarah's surprised brown eyes looked at Fern's face, then down at her hand. Sarah sucked her bottom lip into her mouth for ten seconds, then put her hand down next to Fern's.

They meshed fingers and pressed palm to palm.

Whoever you are, your hand is warm, Fern thought. *And thank you.*

COCKFIGHT

by Jane Yolen

The pit cleaners circled noisily, gobbling up the old fewmets with their iron mouths. They spat out fresh sawdust and moved on. It generally took several minutes between fights and the mechanical clanking of the cleaners was matched by the roars of the pit-wise dragons and the last-minute betting calls of their masters.

Jakkin heard the noises through the wooden ceiling as he groomed his dragon in the under-pit stalls. It was the first fight for both of them and Jakkin's fingers reflected his nervousness. He simply could not keep them still. They picked off bits of dust and flicked at specks on the dragon's already gleaming scales. They polished and smoothed and polished again. The red dragon seemed oblivious to first fight jitters and arched up under Jakkin's hands.

Jakkin was pleased with his dragon's color. It was a dull red. Not the red of the hollyberry or the red of the wildflowering trillium, but the red of life's blood spilt upon the sand. It was a fighter's color, and he had known it from the first. That was why he had sneaked the dragon from its nest, away from its hatchlings, when the young worm had emerged from its egg in the sand of the nursery.

The dragon had looked then like any lizard, for it had not yet shed its eggskin which was wrinkled and

74

yellow, like custard scum. But Jakkin had sensed, beneath the skin, a darker shadow and had known it would turn red. Not many would have known, but Jakkin had, though he was only thirteen.

The dragon was not his, not really, for it had belonged to his master's nursery, just as Jakkin did. But on Austar IV there was only one way to escape from bond, and that was with gold. There was no quicker way to get gold than as a bettor in the dragon-pits. And there was nothing Jakkin wanted more than to be free. He had lived over half his life bonded to the nursery, from the time his parents had died when he was four. And most of that time he had worked as a stall boy, no better than a human pit cleaner, for Sarkkhan's Dragonry. What did it matter that he lived and slept and ate with his master's dragons? He was allowed to handle only their fewmets and spread fresh sawdust for their needs. If he could not raise a fighting dragon himself and buy his way out of bond, he would end up an *old* stall boy, like Likkarn, who smoked blisterweed, dreamed his days away, and cried red tears.

So Jakkin had watched and waited and learned as much as a junior stall boy could about dragon ways and dragonlore for he knew the only way out of bond was to steal that first egg and raise it up for fighting or breeding or, if need was great, for the stews. But Jakkin did not know eggs, could sense nothing through the elastic shell, and so he had stolen a young dragon instead. It was a greater risk, for eggs were never counted but the new-hatched dragons were. At Sarkkhan's

Dragonry old Likkarn kept the list of hatchlings. He was the only one of the bonders who could write, though Jakkin had taught himself to read a bit.

Jakkin had worried all through the first days that Likkarn would know and, knowing, tell. He kept the hatchling in a wood crate turned upside-down way out in the sands. He swept away his footsteps to and from the crate and reckoned his way to it at night by the stars. And somehow he had not been found out. His reward had come as the young worm had grown.

First the hatchling had turned a dull brown and could trickle smoke through its nose slits. The wings on its back, crumpled and weak, had slowly stretched to a rubbery thickness. For days it had remained mud-colored. Another boy might have sold it then to the stews, keeping the small fee in his leather bond bag that swung from the metal bond chain around his neck. It would have been a laughable amount, a coin or two at the most, and the bag would have looked just as empty as before.

But Jakkin had waited and the dragon finally molted, patchworking into a red. The nails on its fore-claws, which had been as brittle as jingle shells, were now as hard as golden oak and the same color. Its hind-claws were dull and strong as steel. Its eyes were two black shrouds and it had not roared yet, but Jakkin knew that roar would come, loud and full and fierce, when it was first blooded in the ring. The quality of the roar would start the betting rippling again through the crowd who judged a fighter by the timbre of its voice.

Jakkin could hear the cleaners clanking out of the ring through the mecho-holes. He ran his fingers through his straight brown hair and tried to swallow, then touched a dimple on his cheek that was as deep as a blood score. His hand found the bond bag and kneaded it several times for luck.

"Soon now," he promised the red dragon in a hoarse whisper, his hand still on the bag. "Soon. We will show them a first fight. They will remember us."

The red was too busy munching on blisterwort to reply.

A disembodied voice announced the next fight. "Jakkin's Red, Mekkle's Bottle O' Rum."

Jakkin winced. He knew a little about Mekkle's dragon already. He had heard about it that morning as they had come into the pit stalls. Dragon masters and trainers did not chatter while they groomed their fighters, but bettors did, gathering around the favorites and trading stories of other fights. Mekkle's Rum was a light-colored male that favored its left side and had won three of its seven fights—the last three. It would never be great, the whispers had run, but it was good enough, and a hard draw for a new dragon, possibly disastrous for a would-be dragon master. Jakkin knew his red could be good with time, given the luck of the draw. It had all the things a dragon fighter was supposed to have: it had heart, it listened well, it did all he asked of it. But just as Jakkin had never run a fighter before, the red had never been in a ring. It had never been blooded or given roar. It did not even have its true name yet. Already, he knew, the betting was way against the young red and he could hear the murmur of new bets after the announcement. The odds would be so awful, he might never be able to get a sponsor for a second match. First fights were free, but seconds cost gold. And if he had no sponsor, that would leave only the stews for the dragon and a return to bond for himself.

Jakkin stroked the bond bag once more, then buttoned his shirt up over it to conceal it. He did not know yet what it felt like to be free, so he could stand more years as a bonder. And there might always be another chance to steal. But how could he ever give up the red to the stews? It was not any old dragon, it was his. They had already shared months of training, long nights together under the Austar moons. He knew its mind better than his own. It was a deep glowing cavern of colors and sights and sounds. He remembered the first time he had really felt his way into it, lying on his side, winded from running, the red beside him, a small mountain in the sand. The red calmed him when he was not calm, cheered him when he thought he could not be cheered. Linked as he was with it now, how could he bear to hear its last screams in the stews and stay sane? Perhaps that was why Likkarn was always yelling at the younger bonders, why he smoked blisterweed that turned the mind foggy and made a man cry red tears. And perhaps that was why dragons in the stews were always yearlings or the untrained. Not because they were softer, more succulent, but because no one would hear them when they screamed.

Jakkin's skin felt slimed with perspiration and the dragon sniffed it on him, giving out a few straggles of smoke from its slits. Jakkin fought down his own fear. If he could not control it, his red would have no chance at all, for a dragon was only as good as its master. He took deep breaths and then moved over to the red's head. He looked into its black, unblinking eyes.

"Thou art a fine one, my Red," he whispered. "First fight for us both, but I trust thee." Jakkin always spoke *thou* to his dragon. He felt, somehow, it brought them closer. "Trust me?"

The dragon responded with slightly rounded smokes. Deep within its eyes Jakkin thought he detected small lights.

"Dragon's fire!" he breathed. "Thou *art* a fighter. I knew it!"

Jakkin slipped the ring from the red dragon's neck and rubbed its scales underneath. They were not yet as hard as a mature fighter's and for a moment he worried that the older Bottle O' Rum might tear the young dragon beyond repair. He pulled the red's head down and whispered into its ear. "Guard thyself here," he said, rubbing with his fingers under the tender neck links and thinking danger at it.

The dragon shook its head playfully and Jakkin slapped it lightly on the neck. With a surge, the red dragon moved out of the stall, over to the dragonlock, and flowed up into the ring.

*   *   *

"It's eager," the whisper ran around the crowd. They always liked that in young dragons. Time enough to grow cautious in the pit. Older dragons often were reluctant and had to be prodded with jumpsticks behind the wings or in the tender underparts of the tail. The bettors considered that a great fault. Jakkin heard the crowd's appreciation as he came up into the stands.

It would have been safer for Jakkin to remain below, guiding his red by mind. That way there would be no chance for Master Sarkkhan to find him here, though he doubted such a well-known breeder would enter a backcountry pit fight. And many trainers, Mekkle being one of them, stayed in the stalls drinking and smoking and guiding their dragons where the crowd could not influence them. But Jakkin needed to see the red as well as feel it, to watch the fight through his own eyes as well as the red's. They had trained too long at night, alone, in the sands. He did not know how another dragon in a real fight would respond. He had to see to understand it all. And the red was used to him being close by. He did not want to change that now. Besides, unlike many of the other bonders, he had never been to a fight, only read about them in books and heard about them from his bond mates. This might be his only chance. And, he further rationalized, up in the stands he might find out more about Mekkle's orange that would help him help the red.

Jakkin looked around the stands cautiously from the stairwell. He saw no one he knew, neither fellow bonders nor masters who had traded with Sarkkhan. He edged quietly into the stands, just one more boy at the fights. Nothing called attention to him but the empty bond bag beneath his shirt. He checked his buttons carefully to make sure they were closed. Then he leaned forward and watched as his red circled the ring.

It held its head high and measured the size of the pit, the height of the walls. It looked over the bettors as if it were counting them, and an appreciative chuckle went through the crowd. Then the red scratched in the sawdust several times, testing its depth. And still Bottle O' Rum had not appeared.

Then with an explosion, Bottle O' Rum came through the dragonlock and landed with all four feet planted well beneath the level of the sawdust, his claws fastened immovably to the boards.

"Good stance," shouted someone in the crowd and the betting began anew.

The red gave a little flutter with its wings, a flapping that might indicate nervousness and Jakkin thought at it: "He is a naught. A stander. But thy nails and wings are fresh. Do not be afraid. Remember thy training." At that the little red's head went high and its neck scales glittered in the artificial sun of the pit.

"Watch that neck," shouted a heckler. "There's one that'll be blooded soon."

"Too soon," shouted another from across the stands at him.

Bottle O' Rum charged the inviting neck.

It was just as Jakkin hoped, for charging from the fighting stance is a clumsy maneuver at best. The claws must be retracted simultaneously, and the younger the dragon the more brittle its claws. The orange, Rum, was seven fights older than the red, but it was not yet mature. As Rum charged, one of the nails on his front right claw caught in the floor-boards and splintered, causing him to falter for a second. The red shifted its position slightly. Instead of blooding the red on the vulnerable neck, Rum's charge brought him headlong onto the younger dragon's chest plates, the hardest and slipperiest part of a fighting dragon's armor. The screech of teeth on scale brought winces to the crowd. Only Jakkin was ready, for it was a maneuver he had taught his dragon out in the hidden sands.

"Now!" he cried out and thought at once.

The young red needed no urging. It bent its neck around in a fast, vicious slash, and blood spurted from behind the ears of Mekkle's Rum.

"First blood!" cried the crowd.

Now the betting would change, Jakkin thought with a certain pleasure, and touched the bond bag through the thin cloth of his shirt. Ear bites bleed profusely but were not important. It would hurt the orange dragon a little, like a pin-prick or a splinter does a man. It would make the dragon mad and—more important—a bit more cautious. But first blood! It looked good.

Bottle O' Rum roared with the bite, loud and piercing. It was too high up in the throat yet with surprising strength. Jakkin listened carefully, trying to judge. He had heard dragons roar at the nursery in mock battles or when the keepers blooded them for customers intent on hearing the timbre before buying. To him the roar sounded as if it had all its power in the top tones and none that resonated. Perhaps he was wrong, but if his red could *outlast* the orange, it might impress this crowd.

In his eagerness to help his dragon, Jakkin moved to the pit rail. He elbowed his way though some older men.

"Here youngster, what do you think you're doing?" A man in a grey leather coverall spoke. He was obviously familiar with the pits. Anyone in leather knew his way around. And his face, what could be seen behind the grey beard, was scored with dragonblood scars.

"Get back up in the stands. Leave ringside to the money men," said his companion, taking in Jakkin's leather-patched cloth shirt and trousers with a dismissing look. He ostentatiously jounced a full bag that hung from his wrist on a leather thong.

Jakkin ignored them, fingering his badge with the facs picture of the red on it. He leaned over the rail. "Away, away good Red," he thought at his dragon and smiled when the red immediately wheeled and winged up from its blooded foe. Only then did he turn and address the two scowling bettors. "Pit right, good Sirs," he said with deference, pointing at the same time to his badge.

They mumbled, but moved aside for him.

The orange dragon in the pit shook its head and the blood beaded its ears like a crown. A few drops spattered over the walls and into the stands. Each place a drop touched burned with that glow peculiar to the acidy dragon's blood. One watcher in the third row of the stands was not quick enough and was seared on the cheek. He reached up a hand to the wound but did not move from his place.

The orange Rum stood up tall again and dug back into the dust.

"Another stand," said the grey leather man to Jakkin's right.

"Pah, that's all it knows," said the dark man beside him.

"That's how it won three fights. Good stance, but that's it. I wonder why I bet it all. Let's go and get something to smoke. This fight's a bore."

Jakkin watched them leave from the corner of his eye, but he absorbed their information. If the orange was a stander, if the information were true, it would help him with the fight.

The red dragon's leap back had taken it to the north side of the pit. When it saw that Bottle O' Rum had chosen to stand, it circled closer warily.

Jakkin thought at it, "He's good in the stance. Do not force him there. Make him come to thee."

The dragon's thoughts, as always, came back clearly to Jakkin wordless but full of color and emotion. The red wanted to charge; the dragon it had blooded was waiting. The overwhelming urge was to carry the fight to the foe.

"No, my Red. Trust me. Be eager, but not foolish," cautioned Jakkin, looking for an opening.

But the crowd, as eager as the young dragon, was communicating with it, too. The yells of the men, their thoughts of charging, overpowered Jakkin's single line of calm. The red started to move.

When it saw the red bunching for a charge, Rum solidified his stance. His shoulders went rigid with the strain. Jakkin knew that if his red dived at that standing rock, it could quite easily break a small bone in its neck. And rarely did a dragon come back to the pit once its neck bones had been set. Then it was good only for the breeding nurseries—if it had a fine pit-record—or the stews.

"Steady, steady," Jakkin said, aloud. Then he shouted and waved a hand, "NO!"

The red had already started its dive, but the movement of Jakkin's hand was a signal too powerful for it to ignore and, at the last possible minute, it pulled to one side. As it passed, Rum slashed at it with a gaping mouth and shredded its wingtip.

"Blood," the crowd roared and waited for the red dragon to roar back.

Jakkin felt its confusion and his head swam with the red of dragon's blood as his dragon's thoughts came to him. He watched as it soared to the top of the building and scorched its wingtip on the artificial sun, cauterizing the wound. Then, still hovering, it opened its mouth for its first blooded roar.

There was no sound.

"A mute!" called a man from the stands. He spit angrily to one side. "Never heard one before."

A wit near him shouted back, "You won't hear this one, either."

The crowd laughed at this, and passed the quip around the stands.

But Jakkin only stared up at his red bitterly. "A mute," he thought at it. "You are as powerless as I."

His use of the distancing pronoun *you* further confused the young dragon, and it began to circle downward in a disconsolate spiral, closer and closer to the waiting Rum, its mind a maelstrom of blacks and greys.

Jakkin realized his mistake in time. "It does not matter," he cried out in his mind. "Even with no roar, thee wilt be great." He said it with more conviction than he really felt, but it was enough for the red. It broke out of its spiral and hovered, wings working evenly.

The maneuver, however, was so unexpected that the pit-wise Bottle O' Rum was bewildered. He came out of his stance with a splattering of dust and fewmets, stopped, then charged again. The red avoided him easily, landing on his back and raking the orange scales with its claws. That drew no blood, but it frightened the older dragon into a hindfoot rise. Balancing on his tail, Rum towered nearly eight feet high, his front claws scoring the air, a single shot of fire streaking from his slits.

The red backwinged away from the flames and waited.

"Steady, steady," thought Jakkin, in control again. He let his mind recall for them both the quiet sands and the cool nights when they had practiced with the wooden dragon-form on charges and clawing. Then Jakkin repeated out loud, "Steady, steady."

A hard hand on his shoulder broke through his thoughts and the sweet-strong smell of blisterweed assailed him. Jakkin turned.

"Not so steady yourself," came a familiar voice.

Jakkin stared up at the ravaged face, pocked with blood scores and stained with tear-lines.

"Likkarn," breathed Jakkin, suddenly and terribly afraid.

Jakkin tried to turn back to the pit where his red waited. The hand on his shoulder was too firm, the fingers like claws through his shirt.

"And how did *you* become a dragon trainer?" the man asked.

Jakkin thought to bluff. The old stall boy was often too sunk in his smokedreams to really listen. Bluff and run, for the wild anger that came after blister-dreams never gave a smoker time to reason. "I found. . . found an egg, Likkarn," he said. And it could be true. There were a few wild dragons, bred from escapes that had gone feral.

The man said nothing but shook his head.

Jakkin stared at him. This was a new Likkarn, harder, full of purpose. Then Jakkin noticed. Likkarn's eyes were clearer than he had ever seen them, no longer the furious pink of the weeder, but a softer rose. He had not smoked for several days at least. It was useless to bluff or run. "I took it from the nursery, Likkarn. I raised it in the sands. I trained it at night, by the moons."

"That's better. Much better. Liars are an abomination," the man said with a bitter laugh. "And you fed it

87

what? Goods stolen from the master, I wager. You born-bonders know nothing. Nothing."

Jakkin's cheeks were burning now. "I am no born-bonder. And I would never steal from the Master's stores. I planted in the sands last year and grew blister-weed and burnwort. I gathered the rest in the swamps. *On my own time*." He added that fiercely.

"Bonders have no time of their own," Likkarn muttered savagely. "And supplements?"

"The Master says supplements are bad for a fighter. They make a fighter fast in the beginning, but they dilute the blood." Jakkin looked into Likkarn's eyes more boldly now. "I heard the Master say that. To a buyer."

Likkarn's smile was wry and twisted. "And you eavesdrop as well." He gave Jakkin's shoulder a particularly vicious wrench.

Jakkin gasped and closed his eyes with the pain. He wanted to cry out, and thought he had, when he realized it was not his own voice he heard but a scream from the pit. He pulled away from Likkarn and stared. The scream was Bottle O' Rum's, a triumphant roar as he stood over the red whose injured wing was pinioned beneath Rum's right front claw.

"*Jakkin . . .*" came Likkarn's voice behind him, full of warning. How often Jakkin had heard that tone right before old Likkarn had roused from a weed dream to the fury that always followed. Likkarn was old, but his fist was still solid.

Jakkin trembled, but he willed his focus onto the red whose thoughts came tumbling back into his head now

88

in a tangle of muted colors and whines. He touched his hand to the small lump under his shirt where the bond bag hung. He could feel his own heart beating through the leather shield. "Never mind, my Red," soothed Jakkin. "Never mind the pain. Recall the time I stood upon thy wing and we played at the Great Upset. Recall it well, thou mighty fighter. Remember. Remember."

The red stirred only slightly and made a flutter with its free wing. The crowd saw this as a gesture of submission. So did Rum and, through him, his Master Mekkle. But Jakkin did not. He knew the red had listened well and understood. The game was not over yet. Pit-fighting was not all brawn; how often Master Sarkkhan had said that. The best fighters, the ones who lasted for years, were cunning gamesters and it was this he had guessed about his red from the first.

The fluttering of the unpinioned wing caught Bottle O' Rum's eye and the orange dragon turned towards it, relaxing his hold by a single nail.

The red fluttered its free wing again. Flutter and feint. Flutter and feint. It needed the orange's attention totally on that wing. Then its tail could do the silent stalking it had learned in the sands with Jakkin.

Bottle O' Rum followed the fluttering as though laughing for his own coming triumph. His dragon jaws opened slightly in a deadly grin. If Mekkle had been in the stands instead of below in the stalls, the trick might not have worked. But the orange dragon, intent on the fluttering wing, leaned his head way back and fully

89

opened his jaws, readying for the kill. He was unaware of what was going on behind him.

"Now!" shouted Jakkin in his mind and only later realized that the entire stands had roared words with him. Only the crowd had been roaring for the wrong dragon.

The red's tail came around with a snap, as vicious and as accurate as a driver's whip. It caught the orange on its injured ear and across an eye.

Rum screamed instead of roaring and let go of the red's wing. The red was up in an instant and leaped for Bottle O' Rum's throat.

One, two and the ritual slashes were made. The orange throat was coruscated with blood and Rum instantly dropped to the ground.

Jakkin's dragon backed at once, slightly akilter because of the wound in its wing.

"Game to Jakkin's Red," said the disembodied voice over the speaker.

The crowd was strangely silent. Then a loud whoop sounded from one voice buried in the stands, a bettor who had taken a chance on the First Fighter.

That single voice seemed to rouse Bottle O' Rum. He raised his head from the ground groggily. Only his head and half his neck cleared the dust. He strained to arch his neck over, exposing the underside to the light. The two red slashes glistened like thin hungry mouths. Then Rum began a strange, horrible humming that changed to a high-pitched whine. His body began to shake and the shaking became part of the sound as the dust eddied around him.

The red dragon swooped down and stood before the fallen Rum, as still as stone. Then, it too, began to shake.

The sound changed from a whine to a high roar. Jakkin had never heard anything like it before. He put his hands to the bond bag, then to his ears.

"What is it? What is happening?" he cried out, but the men on either side of him had moved away. Palms to ears, they backed towards the exits. Many in the crowd had already gone down the stairs, setting the thick wood walks between themselves and the noise.

Jakkin tried to reach the red dragon's mind, but all he felt were storms of orange winds, hot and blinding, and a shaft of burning white light. As he watched, the red rose up on its hind legs and raked the air frantically with its claws as if getting ready for some last deadly blow.

"Fool's Pride," came Likkarn's defeated voice behind him, close enough to his ear to hear. "That damnable dragon wants death. He has been shamed and he'll scream your red into it. Then you'll know. All you'll have left is a killer on your hands. I lost three that way. *Three*. Fool's Pride." He shouted the last at Jakkin's back for at his first words, Jakkin had thrown himself over the railing into the pit. He landed on all fours, but was up and running at once.

He had heard of Fool's Pride, that part of the fighting dragon's bloody past that was not always bred out. Fool's Pride that led some defeated dragons to demand death. It had nearly caused dragons to become extinct. If men had not carefully watched the lines, trained the fighters to lose with grace, there would have been no dragons left on Austar IV. A good fighter should have a love of blooding, yes. But killing made dragons unmanageable, made them feral, made them wild.

Jakkin crashed into the red's side. "No, no," he screamed up at it, beating on its body with his fists. "Do not wet thy jaws in his death." He reached as high as he could and held on to the red's neck. The scales slashed one of his palms, but he did not let go.

It was his touch more than his voice or his thought that stopped the young red. It turned slowly, sluggishly, as if rousing from a dream. Jakkin fell from its neck to the ground.

The movement away shattered Bottle O' Rum's concentration. He slipped from screaming to unconsciousness in an instant.

The red nuzzled Jakkin, its eyes unfathomable, its mind still clouded. The boy stood up. Without bothering to brush the dust from his clothes, he thought at it, *"Thou mighty First."*

The red suddenly crowded his mind with victorious sunbursts, turned, then streaked back through the hold to its stall and the waiting burnwort.

Mekkle and two friends came up the stairs, glowering, leaped into the pit and dragged the fainting orange out through a mecho-hold by his tail.

Only then did Jakkin walk back to ringside, holding his cut hand palm up. It had just begun to sting.

Likkarn, still standing by the railing was already smoking a short strand of blisterweed. He stared blankly as the red smoke circled his head.

"I owe you," Jakkin said slowly up to him, hating to admit it. "I did not know Fool's Pride when I saw it. Another minute and the red would have been good for nothing but the stews. If I ever get a Second Fight, I will give you some of the gold. *Your bag is not yet full.*"

Jakkin meant the last phrase simply as ritual, but Likkarn's eyes suddenly roused to weed fury. His hand went to his throat. "You owe me nothing," said the old man. He held his head high and the agelines on his neck crisscrossed like old fight scars. *"Nothing.* You owe the master everything. I need no reminder that I am a bonder. *I fill my bag myself.*"

Jakkin bowed his head under the old man's assault. "Let me tend the red's wounds. Then do with me as you will." He turned and, without waiting for an answer, ducked through the mecho-hold and slid down the shaft.

Jakkin came to the stall where the red was already at work grooming itself, polishing its scales with a combination of fire and spit. He slipped the ring around its neck and knelt down by its side. Briskly he put his hand out to touch its wounded wing, in a hurry to finish the examination before Likkarn came down. The red drew back at his touch, sending a mauve landscape into his mind, dripping with grey tears.

"Hush little flametongue," crooned Jakkin, slowing himself down and using the lullaby sounds he had invented to soothe the hatchling of the sands. "I won't hurt thee. I want to help."

But the red continued to retreat from him, crouching against the wall.

Puzzled, Jakkin pulled his hand back, yet still the red huddled away, and a spurt of yellow-red fire flamed from its slits. "Not here, furnace-lung," said Jakkin, annoyed. "That will set the stall on fire."

A rough hand pushed him aside. It was Likkarn, no longer in the weed dream but starting into the uncontrollable fury that capped a weed-sequence. The dragon, its mind open with the pain of its wound and the finish of the fight, had picked up Likkarn's growing anger and reacted to it.

"You don't know wounds," growled Likkarn. "I'll show you what a *real* trainer knows." He grabbed the dragon's torn wing and held it firmly, then with a quick motion, and before Jakkin could stop him, he set his mouth on the jagged tear.

The dragon reared back in alarm and tried to whip its tail around, but the stalls were purposely built small to curb such motion. Its tail scraped along the wall and barely tapped the man. But Jakkin grabbed at Likkarn's arm with both hands and furiously tore him from the red's wing.

"I'll kill you, you weeder," he screamed. "Can't you wait till a dragon is in the stews before you try to eat it. I'll kill you." He slammed at Likkarn with his fist and feet, knowing as he did it that the man's weed-anger would be turned on him and he might be killed by it, and not caring. Suddenly Jakkin felt himself being lifted up from behind, his legs dangling, kicking uselessly at the air. A strong arm around his waist held him fast. Another pushed Likkarn back against the wall.

"Hold off, boy. He was a good trainer—once. And he's right about the best way to deal with a wing wound. An open part, filled with dragon's blood, might burn the tongue surely. But a man's tongue heals quickly, and there is something in human saliva that closes these small tears."

Jakkin twisted around as best he could and saw the man he had most feared seeing. It was Master Sarkkhan himself, in a leather suit of the red-and-gold nursery colors. His red beard was brushed and he looked grim.

Sarkkhan put the boy down but held on to him with one hand. With the other, he brushed his hair back from a forehead that was pitted with blood scores as evenly spaced as a bonder's chain. "Now promise me you will let Likkarn look to the red's wing."

"I will not. He's a weeder and he's as likely to rip the red as heal it and the red hates him—just as I do," shouted Jakkin. There he stopped and put the back of his hand over his mouth, shocked at his own bold words.

Likkarn raised his hand to the boy and aimed a blow at his head, but before the slap landed, the dragon nosed forward and pushed the man to the ground.

Master Sarkkhan let go of Jakkin's shoulder, and considered the red for a moment. "I think the boy is right, Likkarn. The dragon won't have you. It's too closely linked. I wouldn't have guessed that, but there it is. Best leave this to the boy and me."

Likkarn got up clumsily and brushed off his clothes. His bond bag had fallen over the top of his overall bib in the scuffle and Jakkin was shocked to see that it was halfway plump, jangling with coins. Likkarn caught his look and angrily stuffed the bag back inside, then jabbed the outline of Jakkin's bag under his shirt with a reddened finger. "And how much have *you* got there, boy?" He walked off with as much dignity as he could muster to slump by the stairwell and watch.

Sarkkhan ignored them both and crouched down by the dragon, letting it get the smell of him. He caressed its jaws and under its neck with his large, scarred hands. Slowly the big man worked his way back towards the wings, crooning at the dragon in low tones, smoothing its scales, all the while staring into its eyes. Slowly the membranes, top and bottom, shuttered the red's eyes and it relaxed. Only then did Sarkkhan let his hand close over the wounded wing. The dragon gave a small shudder but was otherwise quite still.

"Your red did a good job searing its wound on the light. Did you teach it that?"

"No," the boy admitted.

"Of course not, foolish of me. How could you. No light in the sands. Good breeding then," said Sarkkhan with a small chuckle of appreciation. "And I should know. After all, your dragon's mother is my best— Heart O' Mine."

"You . . . you knew all along, then." Jakkin felt as confused as a blooded First.

Sarkkhan stood up and stretched. In the confines of

the stall he seemed enormous, a red-gold giant. Jakkin suddenly felt smaller than his years.

"*Fewmets*, boy, of course I knew," Sarkkhan answered. "I know *everything* that happens at my nursery."

Jakkin collapsed down next to his dragon and put his arm over its neck. When he finally spoke, it was in a very small voice. "Then why did you let me do it? Why did you let me steal the dragon? Were you trying to get me in trouble? Do you want me in gaol?"

The man threw back his head and roared, and the dragons in neighboring stalls stirred uneasily at the sound. Even Likkarn started at the laugh and a trainer six stalls down growled in disapproval. Then Sarkkhan looked down at the boy, crouched by the red dragon. "I'm sorry, boy, I forget how young you are. Never known anyone quite that young to successfully train a hatchling. But every man gets a chance to steal one egg. It's a kind of test, you might say. The only way to break out of bond. Some men are meant to be bonders, some masters. How else can you tell? Likkarn's tried it—endless times, eh, old man?" The master glanced over at Likkarn with a look akin to affection, but Likkarn only glared back. "Steal an egg and try. The only things it is wrong to steal are a bad egg or your master's provisions." Sarkkhan stopped talking for a minute and mused, idly running a hand over the red dragon's back as it chewed contentedly now on its burnwort, little grey straggles of smoke easing from its slits. "Of course most *do* steal bad eggs or are too impatient to train what comes out and instead they make a quick sale to the stews just for a few coins to jangle in their bags. Then it's back to bond again before a month is out. It's only the ones who steal provisions that land in gaol, boy."

"Then you won't put me in gaol. Or the red in the stews? I couldn't let you do that, Master Sarkkhan. Not even you. I wouldn't let you. I . . ." Jakkin began to stutter as he often did in his master's presence.

"Send a First Fighter, a *winner* to the stews? *Fewmets,* boy, where's your brain. Been smoking blisterweed?" Sarkkhan hunkered down next to him.

Jakkin looked down at his sandals. His feet were soiled from the dust of the stall. He ordered his stomach to calm down, and he felt an answering muted rainbow of calm from the dragon. Then a peculiar thought came to him. "Did *you* have to steal an egg, Master Sarkkhan?"

The big red-headed man laughed and thrust his hand right into Jakkin's face. Jakkin drew back but Sarkkhan was holding up two fingers and wiggling them before his eyes.

"Two! I stole two. A male and a female. And it was not mere chance. Even then I knew the difference. *In the egg* I knew. And that's why I'm the best breeder on Austar IV." He stood up abruptly and held out his hand to the boy. "But enough. The red is fine and you are due upstairs." He yanked Jakkin to his feet and seemed at once to lose his friendliness.

"Upstairs?" Jakkin could not think what that meant. "You said I was not to go to gaol. I want to stay with the red. I want . . ."

"*Worm-wort,* boy, have you been listening or not?

You have to register that dragon, give her a name, record her as a First Fighter, a winner."

"*Her?*" Jakkin heard only the one word.

"Yes, a her. Do you challenge *me* on that? And I want to come with you and collect my gold. I bet a bagfull on that red of yours—on Likkarn's advice. He's been watching you train, my orders. He said she was looking good and sometimes I believe him." Sarkkhan moved towards the stairwell where Likkarn still waited. "I owe him you know. He taught me everything."

"Likkarn? Taught you?"

They stopped by the old man who was slumped again in another blisterweed dream. Sarkkhan reached out and took the stringy red weed ash from the old man's hand. He threw it on the floor and ground it savagely into the dust. "He wasn't born a weeder, boy. And he hasn't forgotten all he once knew." Then shaking his head, Master Sarkkhan moved up the stairs, impatiently waving a hand at the boy to follow.

A stray strand of color-pearls passed through Jakkin's mind and he turned around to look at the dragon's stall. Then he gulped and said in a rush at Sarkkhan's back, "But she's a mute, Master. She may have won this fight by wiles, but she's a mute. No one will bet on a dragon that cannot roar."

The man reached down and grabbed Jakkin's hand, yanking him through the doorway and up the stairs. They mounted two at a time. "You really are lizard-waste," said Sarkkhan, punctuating his sentences with another step. "Why do you think I sent a half-blind weeder skulking around the sands at night watching you train a snatchling? Because I'd lost my mind? *Fewmets*, boy. I want to know what is happening to every damned dragon I have bred because I have had a hunch and a hope these past two years, breeding small-voiced dragons together. I've been *trying* to breed a mute. Think of it, a mute fighter—why, it would give nothing away, not to pit foes or to bettors. A mute fighter and its trainer . . ." And Sarkkhan stopped on the stairs, looking down at the boy. "Why, they'd rule the pits, boy."

They finished the stairs and turned down the hallway. Sarkkhan strode ahead and Jakkin had to double-time in order to keep up with the big man's strides.

"Master Sarkkhan," he began at the man's back.

Sarkkhan did not break stride but growled, "I am no longer your master, Jakkin. *You* are a master now. A master trainer. That dragon will speak only to you, go only on your command. Remember that and act accordingly."

Jakkin blinked twice and touched his chest. "But . . . but my bag is empty. I have no gold to fill it. I have no sponsor for my next fight. I . . ."

Sarkkhan whirled, and his eyes were fierce. "*I* am sponsor for your next fight, I thought that much, at least, was clear. And when your bag is full, you will pay me no gold for your bond. Instead I want to pick of the first hatching when the red is bred—to a mate of my choosing. If she is a complete mute, she may breed true, and *I* mean to have it."

"Oh, Master Sarkkhan," Jakkin cried, suddenly realizing that all his dreams were realities, "you may have the pick of the first *three* hatchings." He grabbed the man's hand and tried to shake his thanks into it.

"Fewmets!" the man yelled, startling some of the passers-by. He shook the boy's hand loose. "How can you ever become a bettor if you offer it all up front. You have to disguise your feelings better than that. Offer me the pick of the *third* hatching. Counter me. Make me work for whatever I get."

Jakkin said softly, testing, "The pick of the third."

"First two," said Sarkkhan, softly back and his smile came slowly. Then he roared, "Or I'll have you in gaol and the red in the stews."

A crowd began to gather around them, betting on the outcome of the uneven match. Sarkkhan was a popular figure at pit-fights and the boy was leather-patched, obviously a bonder, an unknown, worm-waste.

All at once Jakkin felt as if he were at pitside. He felt the red's mind flooding into his, a rainbow effect that gave him a rush of courage. It was a game, then, all a game. And he knew how to play. "The second," said Jakkin, smiling back. "After all, Heart's Blood is a First Fighter, and a winner. And," he hissed at Sarkkhan so that only the two of them could hear, "she's a mute." Then he stood straight and said loudly so that it carried to the crowd. "You'll be lucky to have pick of the second."

Sarkkhan stood silently as if considering both the boy and the crowd. He brushed his hair back from his

101

forehead, then nodded. "Done," he said. "A hard bargain." Then he reached over and ruffled Jakkin's hair and they walked off together.

The crowd, settling their bets, let them through.

"I *thought* you were a good learner," Sarkkhan said to the boy. "Second it is. Though," and he chuckled and said quietly, "you should remember this. There is never anything good in a first hatching. Second is the best by far."

"I didn't know," said Jakkin.

"Why should you?" countered Sarkkhan. "*You* are not the best breeder on Austar IV. I am. But I like the name you picked. Heart's Blood out of Heart O' Mine. It suits."

They went through the doorway together to register the red and to stuff Jakkin's bag with hard-earned dragon's gold.

HELLO, DARLING

by Anne Mazer

H ello, darling, it's me."

I looked up from my book and saw a girl dressed in jeans, sneakers, and a ripped T-shirt. A big gray cap was pulled down over her face—all I could see was a firm chin and a bit of straight red hair.

She pulled out a chair. "Haven't seen you in ages, have I? So, tell me, what's new? Anything happening?"

"Not much," I said, wondering who she was and where I had met her. At school? The mall? Baseball practice? Or had I seen her in this library last week?

"Well!" she exclaimed. "I wish I could say the same."

Her friendly voice was irresistible. "You've been busy?"

"All day and all night. Not a moment's rest. It's work, work, work all the time. I can't catch my breath, darling."

I shut my book and sat up in my chair. "Isn't there a law against that?"

"Well, there may be laws, but who pays any attention to them?"

She pushed back the gray cap. She had large blue eyes and a snub nose. Now that I could see her face clearly, she didn't look any more familiar than before.

"Do you ever go to school?" I asked.

"Do I ever!"

"Whose class?"

"Miss Kink, Mr. Bonk, Mrs. Blink, Ms. Funk . . ."

"Kink, Bonk, Blink, and Funk? Never heard of them!"

She rubbed her cheek with the back of her hand. "You ought to be glad you haven't. The worst teachers in the school. They pile on the work—and no excuses allowed. You have to do it every day—or else. And then, when I get home—more, more, more!"

"Oh, no," I said. "Shouldn't you report that to the school guidance counselor?"

"Look at my hands!" She held them in front of my face. They were large, capable-looking hands marked with stars, triangles, half-moons. On her left thumb was a lizard drawn in green ink.

"What's that?"

"My homework assignments for just one night! And I haven't even shown you my feet!"

She kicked off her sneakers. Her big toe had a winged snake winding down it. Her other toes were marked with suns and heads of queens, which nodded slowly as I stared at them.

Little tongues of fire licked at her heels.

"*This* is why I'm up all night," she announced. "Now do you understand, darling?"

"What kind of assignments are these?" I asked.

"Bonk says they're elementary. Funk says they're primary. Blink doesn't say much—she just piles on the work. Kink is a kidder and cracks a joke when I tell her I haven't slept for eighteen days."

"No one can go without sleep for eighteen days!"

"It's tough," she agreed. "Especially when we're not allowed to go home until we finish our assignment."

"You're not allowed to go home?"

"Rules, darling. You know them as well as I."

"I've never heard of them."

"Well, you will. Everyone does, sooner or later."

I cleared my throat. "You go to *this* school?"

"Of course, darling. You see me all the time—don't you?"

"Well, actually . . . no."

Her eyes lit up. "Perhaps I conjured you?"

"I don't think so."

"Ensorcelled you?"

I shook my head.

"Wished you? Dreamt you? Redeemed you?"

"Uh-uh."

"Well, then I must have found you," she said, wiping her hands on her jeans. "There's no other explanation possible."

"I'm not lost," I said.

"Have you ever been?" she asked.

"No!" I said.

"You've never been found?"

"You don't just find people—unless you know them already. These things don't happen here."

She looked thoughtful. "They don't do they?"

"No."

"Never ever?"

"Absolutely not."

She pushed back a strand of lank red hair. Then suddenly she flung out her arms and began to dance.

"I've done it! I've done it!" she cried. "Hooray for me! Just wait till I tell Blink, Funk, Bonk, and Kink! No more homework! I've finally done it!"

"What have you done?" I asked.

"Why, I've created your world," she answered.

I laughed loudly. "Created my world? That's ridiculous."

"Don't be silly, darling. It's done all the time."

She closed her eyes. Another set of eyes were drawn on the lids, and the pupils moved from right to left, from left to right.

"Open your eyes!" I said.

She opened them. There were small spinning globes inside her eye sockets.

She blinked and they disappeared.

I stared at her, speechless.

"This is what I've been working on in class all year. You were my homework assignment. You wouldn't believe how hard it was, darling. But now I can graduate!"

She twirled around the room again. "I'm deliriously happy. I've *finally* done it."

"So," I said, trying to understand, "you're saying you created me . . . and my teachers?"

"Of course. Since preschool."

"I don't believe you."

"Remember Miss Adams, Mrs. Stanton, Mrs. Fulmer, Mr. May . . ."

"Anyone could find out their names," I protested.

"What about your parents?" she said. "Your father is an architect who likes ice-cream bars for breakfast. Your mother works in a bank and has a twitch at the corner of her mouth when she gets angry. And you have a sister, too. I thought of everything. She carries mice on her shoulder when your mother isn't around. Wasn't that a clever touch? It's these little details that earn the best grades."

"Our house. You didn't create our house."

"Oh yes, I did," she said. "From the blue velvet couch to the dust under the refrigerator. And the china dishes and the bunk beds and the blackberry bushes in the backyard."

"What about the shopping mall, the movie theater? What about the library? The highway? The bowling alley? The banks, the factory, the airport?"

"I created them all. Didn't I do a good job? I'll probably graduate with honors."

"My books, my friends, my games!" I was yelling now. "My stories! The pictures I draw! My dreams!"

"All mine, darling. All mine."

I wanted to reason with her, tell her how wrong she was. I wanted to name every person I had ever met. But somehow the names, even my own name, would not come to my lips.

"I don't believe you," I said again. I was trembling with anger and fear. "It can't be!"

"Darling, I really have to go now. It's been so good having this chat with you . . . Perhaps we'll do it again soon."

I jumped up. My hands and feet began to tingle. I looked down at them. Was it my imagination, or were they fading at the edges?

She picked up her sneakers and slung them over her shoulder, then yanked the gray cap over her face.

"Wait!" I shouted.

"Good-bye, darling!"

TRADING PLACES

by Noreen Doyle

At about three hours past noon one summer day (local time, local season), we accidentally destroyed the Auds' *begdim*. When I say "we," I don't mean my sister Marzi and me. I mean "we" like Terrans mean "we."

And when I say "accidentally," I mean like we didn't even know it was there. You can't see a *begdim*. Well, you can, but it doesn't look different from any other piece of land on Audor. An Aud has to tell you it's there, so we just didn't know. They didn't tell us.

There are a lot of things the Auds didn't tell us.

I felt sorry for the Auds. Here they are one day, thinking their *begdim* is . . . well, just that it *is*. The next day, there's a prefabricated Terran building sitting in the middle of it. After all, *begdims* are maybe the most important place to Auds, after their towns. *Begdims* are their trading places.

"The Auds think we're offering to trade the Interstellar Communications Center! Well, we did leave it in their *begdim*, after all. That's what the Auds do when they want to trade something away—leave it in the *begdim*," my older sister Marzi told me, laughing and almost wringing her hands with glee.

She liked that the colony leaders had gotten themselves into trouble with the Auds; Marzi always cheered for the aliens, even in the three-dees where the aliens were bug-

eyed villains. Maybe she had to. She was in her prelimi-
nary courses to become an anthropologist. She was supposed to know all about the local aliens, the Auds. She
certainly sounded as if she knew all about them, but that
was just the way Marzi was about everything.

I guess she was right this time, because the Auds brought
us herds of their shaggy livestock and carts heaped high
with the very best embroidered cloth. We didn't take any of
it, of course. We couldn't give them the I-Comm Center, not
even if they offered us every shaggy gepple and every bolt
of tu-cloth on the planet! This upset the Auds a lot.

Seven citizens from Lalish, the nearest town, protested
at the colony gate. They weren't especially threatening-
looking. Auds tend to be tall but slender, and look very
human except for their wedge-shaped faces and the black
stubble of hair that grows down the center of their skull
and around their shoulders. Our anthropologists went out
and talked to them as best they could.

Because she couldn't go, Marzi sulked and watched
them from the balcony.

"Look at them, Sis! They can scarcely talk to the Auds,"
Marzi said in disgust. "Every Aud town has its own language, as different from each other as English is from
Chinese. Terrans have been on Audor for fifteen years, and
they still barely know even the Lalishi language."

Marzi didn't really think of herself of as Terran, and
neither did I. After all, unlike our parents, we were both
born on Audor and had never seen Old Earth. We felt a
little like aliens ourselves.

"What do you suppose they're doing, then?" I asked.

"They're apologizing, or trying to, anyway." Either Marzi could read lips or she just knew what the anthropologists should be saying, because she was taking courses. "They're telling the Auds that no, we can't take down the I-Comm Center. They're asking if the Auds can't find somewhere else for their *begdim*."

Whether or not Marzi was right about what the anthropologists were saying, the Auds from Lalish did exactly that: picked another *begdim*.

Auds are independent folk. They don't even deal with Auds from other towns very often and don't even know each others' languages. The only word shared by all the Aud languages (according to Marzi) is *begdim*: "trading place." Every town is self-sufficient; they rely on no one else for whatever they need to eat or to shelter themselves. They're proud of that, too. I think they look down on us Terrans because starships bring us things that we can't make for ourselves just yet.

But it's not that the Auds never have contact with outsiders. Each town takes care of its own citizens' needs. The *begdim* takes care of their *wants*.

Even though we'd just ruined their *begdim*, the Lalishi invited us Terrans to the *begdim ul*. This is the ceremony that turns an ordinary piece of land into a *begdim*, so everyone will know where it is. And that included us. Now the Auds hoped we wouldn't go putting a landing strip or a fission plant on it. Not that we'd want to do anything with this piece of land, anyway: it was a forested gully with a creek that flooded every spring. Not the ideal *begdim*, maybe, but it sure was out of our way.

Marzi made sure that I—that anyone who could hear her—realized this. "See how considerate the Auds are? They don't want us to embarrass ourselves again."

The anthropologists and everyone else agreed with her. Maybe they didn't want to argue, or maybe they'd known this all along and just hadn't ever seen a reason to say it aloud. Marzi never needed a reason to say anything.

We weren't the only ones the Lalishi invited to the *begdim ul*. Little caravans came from all over the countryside. Ships with two square sails moored in the bay, and their crews put to shore. They traveled on foot or astride slender, shaggy gepples, laden down with sacks and baskets and barrels.

Everyone settled down around the *begdim*. We Terrans joined them, camping out like everyone else, although we were less than ten minutes by hover from the colony.

Even Marzi had never seen anything like this. For most of the morning she scarcely said more than "Ah!" and "Look!" and "Fascinating!" The only Auds we'd ever seen in person were from Lalish. And here were Auds from twenty or thirty different places, each town distinguishing itself from the others by a special headdress, shoes, or jewelry. Lalishi wear lots of orange and blue and feathers.

It was a festive morning. Everyone cooked their own breakfast, and no one shared any food. We were warned about that; to offer something to an Aud meant that you thought he was asking. And Auds don't ask for anything.

So we ate and watched the Auds eat and wondered when the real ceremony would begin. I got bored. Marzi wouldn't play *Dreadnought* with me on our palmtops—

she insisted on taking notes. So I played by myself.

Finally, seven citizens of Lalish walked down to the bottom of the gully. All the Auds became quiet and put out their fires. Marzi kicked my leg and took away my palmtop. She did not stop taking notes on her own.

The Lalishi laid baskets near the shallow creek. From one basket they took a blanket, which they unfolded. From other baskets they took strings of fat blue beads and carved bits of horn, and tiny little clay bottles probably filled with herbs (or so Marzi said later that day). When they had finished, they retreated up the hill.

One by one, representatives of the other Aud towns came down and did the same. Finally, the mayor of our colony went down. She laid out knives of hard steel, mirrors, perfume, and waterproof cloaks.

When the mayor had rejoined us, the Auds took turns going into the *begdim* again. They would take something from another's pile and replace it with something of their own.

"The Auds have traded that way for centuries, maybe millennia," Marzi whispered, fingering her observations into her palmtop. "Silent barter."

For the rest of the morning and all afternoon, this went on. It was like watching a chess match: objects changed from one pile to the next, every Aud trying to get all he could without offending his trading partners. Marzi was keeping score; she clucked her tongue when someone gave up a pretty blanket for a rusty iron frying pan, but praised the sharp-eyed Aud who noticed the pitcher filled with ripe vetterberries.

114

"Next spring, they'll have their very own vetter patch!" she said. That was an exciting thought. Vetterberries are sweet and tart and buttery.

By dusk, everyone's pile was rearranged.

Everyone's, that is, but ours.

Not a single Aud had taken anything from our pile. So we had taken nothing from any of theirs.

During the night, the Auds carried their newly traded goods far from the *begdim*. By morning, the caravans and ships were gone. It was as if they had never been there at all.

While no one forgot the *begdim ul*, what had happened there didn't mean much to anyone except Marzi, who made an enormous mystery of it all. Finally the anthropologists (and Marzi) agreed that the Auds were shaming us for having ruined their old *begdim*, which was much nicer than the new.

But I liked the new *begdim*. The old begdim was a big meadow that overlooked the ocean; it was wide and open. This new trading place was cozy and almost secret.

And Marzi liked it because it gave her a chance to be near Aud things without being near Auds, which we really weren't supposed to do without an adult around. Marzi was older than I, but nobody ever called her an adult, which annoyed her to no end.

Up the hills a little ways, the creek passes through a little swamp, and Marzi and I often went there to catch toomies. Toomies look something like Terran frogs but they have hard shells. For only a couple of days out of the year they're not poisonous to humans, so that's the time to catch them, of course. Only vetterberries come close to tasting better than toomies, and I'm sorry that you've probably never tried either one.

On one of those toomy-days, we went up to catch some for supper. We snagged eight and stowed them in my cooler-creel at a perfect four degrees centigrade.

On our way home, we walked along the ridge above the *begdim*. It's not taboo or anything; anyone can walk into a *begdim* any time they like, when barter isn't going on. And it wasn't.

But as we walked through the shade of the trees, we noticed Auds watching us from the other side of the gully.

"What are they doing here? I thought they came here only to trade," I said.

"Maybe that's what they're here to do," Marzi replied, and almost immediately the Auds proved her right.

I wasn't surprised. Marzi always knew, especially about aliens. And most especially about Auds.

When they reached the creek, we could see that they were Lalishi, dressed in orange and blue trousers and tunics.

They laid down a basket and disappeared back into the forest.

"What's that all about?" I asked.

"Let's find out," Marzi said. I didn't have any choice but to keep up with her. It was strange, being so near the Auds; I wanted to be beside someone—even someone who wasn't quite an adult.

"They must want to trade with us."

I asked, "But why with us? Our people destroyed

their last *begdim*. And they didn't want anything to do with us at the *begdim ul*."

"Well," Marzi said thoughtfully, "you and I didn't have anything to do with building the I-Comm Center. Maybe the Auds want to trade with the new generation! We're the first humans born on Audor, after all."

It made sense. Marzi was one of those people who always made sense, or at least seemed to. I admire her for that, even if she did talk too much. We stood side by side in the *begdim*, staring at the basket. Inside was a piece of sod, neatly dug up.

"We're supposed to trade for dirt?" I said, wondering if maybe one of the plants in the sod was a flower or some new crop they were giving us. I thought about vetterberries, and my mouth watered.

"Give me your creel."

"My creel?" I shrieked, clutching it to my stomach. Marzi punched me in the shoulder. "But our toomies!"

"We can always catch more toomies." She slipped the strap of the cooler-creel off my shoulder.

"No, we can't," I said, and it was true, but I didn't argue. You can't argue with someone who's always right.

It was the most pathetic looking bit of silent barter I'd ever heard of. The Auds probably ate toomies every day (they weren't ever poisoned by toomies) and we certainly didn't need a basket filled with dirt.

Well, if the Auds didn't like what they saw, they would take away from their own pile. (I imagined them taking back the basket and offering just a pile of dirt.) If the trade was good enough, they would take what we'd left.

When the Auds came back, however, they did neither. They took away nothing, but went back to wait in
the forest.

"What's wrong?" I asked. "They must want us to up
our offer. But why not just take something of their own
away?"

"Maybe they want to talk."

She talked me into letting her go down alone, although I thought it was crazy and I told her it was
crazy. She didn't think it was crazy, and she sounded, as
always, completely, utterly right.

"The Auds won't ever go into the *begdim* with you
sitting down there," I said.

Marzi replied in her best I'm-almost-an-anthropolo-
gist tone, "Yes, they will."

And they did.

One took my creel filled with toomies. Another took
Marzi by the hand.

She turned around and looked for me. I stepped out
of the forest—ran, really, but never made it down the
hill because she held up her hand.

"They want ambassadors!" Marzi called.

"How would you know? You can't speak Lalishi!
Besides, you're too young to be an ambassador!"

"Young people would learn languages better than
adults, maybe. That how it works even with humans."

"But they're not human."

"They seem human enough to me. I'll be back, but
I'm *going*, Sis."

And she did.

I stood there gaping like an idiot as they led her off into the forest. I started to run home, but remembered the basket. Maybe it had a clue, I thought, as to what the Auds were up to.

So I went down into the *begdim*, grabbed the basket, and ran as fast as I could. But not home. The I-Comm Center was closer.

Twigs slapped my face as I ran through the forest, as if the whole planet was trying to tell me *Slap!* What an idiot you are *Slap!* for letting *Slap!* your big sister *Slap!* go off with aliens *Slap! Slap! Slap!*

At last I burst into the meadow. The I-Comm Center was several hundred meters away, and it felt like I'd never get there. I ran, yelling and waving one arm, hoping to catch the attention of the comm-crew in the watch tower.

Sure enough, I did. I wasn't halfway across the Aud's old *begdim* when the service door opened and a hover zipped out.

"The Auds!" I was screaming. "The Auds! They have—"

I tripped, and the next thing I knew two of the comm-crew were kneeling beside me. I tried to get up, to lead them back to the new *begdim*, but a terrible pain shot up from my foot.

"Take it easy. You're Alace Tarcini, right?" said Lieutenant Hassan, holding me down. "You've just broken your ankle, Alace. We'll get you right to the Medicos."

"Well! It looks like the Auds might be interested in trading with us again," Sergeant Luger said to the

119

captain, handing the basket back to me. "Where did you get the basket, Alace?"

"The *begdim*! Where's the dirt that was in the basket?"

"The dirt? It must have fallen out. Here it is." Sergeant Luger bent down and picked up the clod of soil bound up in the roots of plants. He put it back into the basket.

I looked at my ankle. It was terribly swollen, as big as a melon, and bruised and purplish. Nearby was the hole I'd tripped in. It wasn't a big hole. Just about the size of the basket, in fact. . . .

Could it be? I didn't really want to know, but I had to. I picked up the clump of sod and dropped it into the hole. It fit.

The Auds had dug up the soil from their old *begdim* and offered it to us in their new *begdim*.

They were offering us their old trading place, and a creel full of toomies hadn't been a good enough trade.

But we *did* meet the Auds' price, with my sister.

We never saw Marzi alive again.

I said there were a lot of things that the Auds didn't tell us. And to be honest, there were a lot of things we had just never bothered to ask.

THE SEA TURNED UPSIDE DOWN

by Gus Grenfell

Skyreader was troubled. The sky was white, as it should be at this time, but she had the feeling that all was not well.

Nothing else seemed to share her unease. The Burrowers were still burrowing, making their tunnels and piling the red-brown earth in neat piles on the surface. The Hoppers still hopped, the Runners still ran, the Floaters floated, the Swimmers swam, and the Fliers flew. All seemed perfectly content, unaware of anything that might disrupt or affect their activity in any way.

They relied on her, of course. That was why she had been made Skyreader, because she could interpret the signs. She was sensitive to the slightest changes—a subtle discoloration, a faint darkening—which told of the approach of a storm above the sky. She could warn them. They all had their hiding places where they would be safe until the danger had passed.

She looked up again. It was time for the pink phase to begin. Sure enough, a faint blush was forming at the edges. It would creep forward until it took over the whole sky. Why was she worried? There were no visible signs. This was a different kind of danger and she didn't understand it. So how could she persuade the others?

The ship touched down and Fraser Barrett filed another notch on the side of his bunk with a smile of satisfaction.

His twentieth new world. This was something special. Maybe they would call this one "Barrett" after him. He was eager to get out and explore.

He called to his Number Two. "Greg! Get yourself suited up. I want you out there with me."

Greg Pienkowsky's face appeared on screen. "Have you checked the atmosphere?"

Fraser requested a readout from the remote sensors on the ship's hull. There was hydrogen and oxygen, but also a poisonous cocktail of other gasses in which arsenic seemed to play a prominent part.

Greg looked at it, too. "No life, then?" he asked.

Fraser shook his head. He'd just about given up hoping to find signs of life. Apart from Earth, the whole galaxy seemed to be a hostile environment.

He checked the temperature: three degrees Celsius. And gravity was about half a G. At least they would be comfortable. On some of the extreme worlds, you took your life in your hands when you went outside the ship, even with the protection of the suits. But the rules said you had to set foot on a planet in order to claim it, so you did.

"I get a good feeling about this place, Greg," Fraser said. "I'd like to take samples from several different locations. We might strike lucky."

What Fraser dreamed of was what he called "the gold mine in the sky." If he found anything worth mining on any of the planets he discovered, and the commercial companies moved in, he was guaranteed a percentage. That's what was going to make him rich.

123

Down on the surface, Fraser planted the United Space Corps flag, in full view of the tracking camera on the ship, while Greg set up a drill to obtain a core sample of the substrata.

They had landed on a wide plain with a depression in the center, and low hills defining a roughly circular edge. Everything was a rusty red color, not unlike Mars, and lit by a weak, pinky-orange sun. The plain was about a half-mile across, probably the result of a meteor impact. The pictures they had seen on their approach showed similar features on other parts of the surface, but not much else, mainly because dense swirls of purple clouds obscured about thirty percent of the world.

As planets went, it didn't look particularly exciting on the surface. But, in some ways, that was an advantage—it made it easier to concentrate on the important geological survey work.

The dip in the center of the plain was about fifty yards away. Fraser bounded over to see what it was like.

"Hey, Greg!" he shouted. "Take a look at this!"

Greg quickly joined him.

Fraser pointed down. The depression was steep-sided and about fifty feet deep. In the bottom was a clear pool of liquid reflecting the sun, which was almost directly overhead.

Greg looked at Fraser, his eyebrows raised. "Water?"

Was there the vaguest hint of a shadow down near the horizon? Skyreader wasn't sure, but, if anyone asked

124

her, that is what she would tell them. The feeling of foreboding wouldn't go away. She would have to take action now.

First she went to the Burrowers.

"Stop!" she said. "There is danger approaching."

They didn't question; they merely did as she said. They curled up and stuck themselves to the tunnel walls with a secretion from glands under their skin.

The Hoppers tethered themselves to the tall grasses among which they lived, by their long spring-like tails. They would bend and sway with the grasses until the commotion was finished.

The Floaters had a similar way of fixing themselves to weeds in the water, while the Swimmers wedged themselves in cracks and crevices of underwater rocks.

The Runners had homes hollowed out of the hill-sides. They ran home and blocked themselves in.

Only the Fliers were reluctant to stop.

"What's the matter, Skyreader?" they said. "The sky is clear. We know. We can get nearer to the top of it than you can."

Skyreader was scornful. "But you can't read the signs! If you could, you'd all be skyreaders. You just ignore them, because you haven't a brain among you. You just flutter around as though nothing in the world could possibly go wrong."

At length, reluctantly, they gave in and clustered together in a tight ball inside a thick, hollow stem.

Satisfied that she had done all she could, Skyreader tied herself to a jutting rock out in the open, where she could see what happened and know as soon as the trouble was over. She wrapped the silk from her spinnerets round and round until she was secure.

"It may look like water," said Fraser, "but so do a lot of things. Still, can't do any harm to test it."

They slithered down the slope to the pool's edge and Greg dipped a bottle into it. When the glass container was half full, he withdrew and corked it.

"There," he said, lifting it up to the light. "It still looks like water. I'll analyze it when we get back to the ship."

Greg couldn't contain his excitement when he had finished the analysis. He let out a whoop.

"Hey, Fraser!" he called out. "It really *is* water. *Pure* water. So pure you could drink it." He passed the flask to his captain.

Fraser looked dubious. "Drink it?"

"Yeah. You agreed the atmosphere couldn't support life, so there's nothing to contaminate it. Chemically, it's fine."

Fraser lifted the flask to eye level. Was it his imagination, or could he see tiny bits floating about in it?

"Better safe than sorry," he said, and popped a sterilizing tablet into the water. He watched it fizz and dissolve. Then he raised the flask to his lips and drank.

"It tastes good," he said, feeling its coolness trickle down his throat.

Things were happening beyond the sky that had never happened before. It didn't change color, but the commotion began and it was worse than ever. The world rocked, shook and tossed about like a Swimmer's egg caught in a river current.

Patches of darkness moved across the sky, then it went completely dark, then so bright it hurt her eyes. When was the horror going to end? Skyreader was in despair.

There were strange sounds, too—deep rumblings far beyond the top of the sky. Then there was another sound: a loud hissing, fizzing noise which seemed to come from everywhere, and the too-bright sky began to wink and sparkle.

Then the sky split.

The outside came tumbling in like the sea turned upside down. There was nothing to stop it. The sky bubble which kept them all alive, which made it possible for them all to live, had gone.

Skyreader cut herself free with her sharp mandibles, but, before she could do anything to save herself, everything became dark again. She could feel herself falling, still surrounded by swirling water. This must be the end, she thought. The end of her and the end of the world.

But the falling suddenly stopped, and Skyreader found herself floating and bobbing, not sinking and drowning. Where was she? It was difficult to breathe, but not impossible. She was just grateful to be alive.

The end of her abdomen began to glow, a pale green glimmer in the darkness that allowed her to examine her surroundings. She had splashed down on the surface of a thick and lumpy "sea" which bubbled and gurgled around her. The air was warm and moist, with an unpleasant, gassy smell. The sky was black.

There was plenty of life around—Swimmers and Floaters. She wondered how far the sea stretched, whether there were other forms of life, whether any others from her old world had survived. She didn't like this world too much, but surely it was better to be alive than dead.

How long would the sky remain black? She stared up into the darkness, looking for signs, and wondered if the teeming population around her needed a skyreader.

Fraser's features contorted sharply as a sharp jab of pain raced through his insides.

"Oofff," he mumbled, holding a hand to his churning stomach.

"You okay?" Greg asked. "If I made some mistake in the analysis . . ."

Fraser shrugged and tried to force a smile, but it came out more like a pained grimace. "Well, you know what they always say about visiting new places," he said.

Greg shook his head. "No. What do they say?"

"Don't drink the water," Fraser replied, feeling his stomach rumble again. "You never know what's in it . . ."

WHOOO-OOO, FLUPPER!

by Nicholas Fisk

This world is called Positos VI PH. Wow, how I used to hate it!

"We're *prisoners!*" I'd shout. "Never allowed out of this crummy unit!"

"And if we *did* get out, what would we *do?*" squeaked Lollo, my sister. She even waved her fists, which was pretty useless as she's only nine and small for her age. I'm nearly twelve.

We stared out of the unit's window. What did we see? A sort of gray-green blancmange, with some dirty yellow prehistoric-looking trees sticking out. And that's all. "I hate you," muttered Lollo.

I said nothing. What was there to say about Positos VI PH? The name tells you everything. The "VI" means it's a sixth-order world—the smallest sort, the dregs. The "PH" means "partly hostile." In other words, it has a tendency to kill humans. Charming.

"Let's play with the video," I said.

"I'm sick of the video."

"Chess, then."

"You'll only win." She chewed her lower lip for some time, then said, "I'm going out."

"You're not! It's not allowed!"

"I'm going *out*," she repeated. I tried to stop her but she kept putting on more and more outside gear. Even her helmet, although Positos air is breathable. Thick and muggy and smelly, but breathable.

I found myself doing what she was doing—donning boots, suit, bleeper, and three sorts of weapons. It's no good arguing with Lollo. Anyhow, I'm supposed to take care of her. Big brother.

"We're off," she said. Off we went. We followed the tracks of our parents' Ruffstuff at first—the wide, deep tracks of its go-anywhere wheels. Mum and Dad are prospectors. They keep searching for something—anything—to sell back home on Earth. It's a hard way to make a living.

The Ruffstuff's tracks swept off to the right so we kept walking to the left. We didn't want to meet them. We'd get told off. After a time, I said, "Look, Lollo, that's enough. Let's go home." But she just marched on.

We came to the swamp.

Today, it's known as Lollo's Lagoon because she saw it first. "Lagoon" is a bit grand: it's really just a big old swamp, surrounded by droopy trees with their roots half in and half out of the water. And big, mossy, fungus-like growths here and there on the shores. We stood and looked at it. Lollo made a face. I broke off a piece of wood or whatever it is from a tree, if that's a tree, and flung it at one of the huge pancake things like giant water-lily leaves that floated on the surface of the water. There was a damp *plaff!* as the soggy wood hit the soggy pancake. "Good shot!" I was about to say—

When it moved! It rose! It reared up! It sort of humped

up in the middle, sucking water with it, shrugging sprays of water from its wavy edges! It was alive!

It took off! Its fringe, its edges, became folded-over hydroplanes. The humped-up middle part was clear of the water. It made an upside-down U shape. Its fringes rippled and it moved. I mean, really *moved*. I fell over backward in the slimy mud.

At first it just zoomed along, hydroplaning. But it had another trick up its sleeves. Suddenly the water inside the hollow of the U seemed to *boil*. Somewhere inside itself, the thing had a sort of jet propulsion.

Now it didn't just move. It accelerated like one of those old twentieth-century water-speed-record breakers and *hurtled* over the water! It swept around in a huge curve. Lollo's mouth hung open. I gaped. It went so fast, we couldn't believe it. Then *hiss!—surge!—vroom!*—it headed straight for us like a thousand-mile-an-hour nightmare!

Now we were both on our backsides in the mud. But just as we thought it was going to flatten us, it somehow backpedaled, cut its jets, rippled its fringes, and turned pink. We stared at it and it seemed to stare at us.

Silence. Then the thing said, "Whooo."

Lollo whooed right back at it. I added a shaky whoo of my own.

The thing—it must have been five meters across—rippled its flanges invitingly and eased right to where we stood. It said, "Whooo?"

You can guess what happened next. Lollo climbed aboard the thing. Her big brave brother followed. The thing said, "Whooo!" and moved.

When we lived Earthside, Lollo and I tried everything: zeta-powered bikes, dune zoomers, no-grav gymnastics, the lot.

You can keep them all as long as you leave us Flupper.

Riding Flupper was Glory, Glory, Glory all the way. Not just the thrill of all that acceleration, all that speed, all that flying water. He was so *nice* about everything. He *wanted* us to be happy aboard him. He showed us the whole lagoon (it is very big), slowing down to let us see the most interesting parts, then hurtled off amid boiling clouds of spray to give us a thrill. He even realized that we might slide off him when he accelerated, and provided us with a vine, like a rope, to hang on to. He held on to the other end, it went underneath him.

Mum and Dad didn't find out about Flupper and us for more than a week. We faked the unit's video to show us "in." That was our only fear—being found out, being told "No. Never again." Meanwhile, Flupper showed us the deadly thorn bushes that wrapped round their prey like octopuses, then whooshed us off at savage speeds—sometimes so fast he aquaplaned over the water.

There were other Flupper-type lily pads, of course. They seemed to welcome us too. We called one the Clown because he used to follow Flupper, cutting him up and teasing him. All in fun, naturally. Flupper would pretend to skid and go out of control, it was terrific—we'd hang on like grim death to the rope.

We knew we were perfectly safe, of course. But we were wrong.

That day, we were on Flupper doing about a million miles an hour. The Clown was racing alongside and Lollo and I were showing off to him, whooing and waving. Lollo raised one leg and waggled her foot cheekily. Her other foot slipped.

She fell down. The rushing water clutched at one of her legs. The pull of the water tore her off Flupper. For a second I glimpsed her wet, frightened face: then she was hurtling away from me, bouncing over the water like a rag doll, her arms and legs flailing.

She hit the blancmange of the shoreline, bounced over it, and flew sprawling into some bushes. Poison thorn bushes.

She screamed. Loudly at first, then in an awful breathless sobbing way.

Flupper took me to the shore and I ran to Lollo. When I reached her, I stopped dead, appalled by what I saw. She was *red*, red all over. The thorns were cutting her to pieces. The bush wrapped itself tighter and tighter around her and the thorns kept going in.

Then the snake thing came. I had seen the snake things from a distance. This one had a pronglike dagger in its head. I was screaming at Flupper and dancing about in an agony of uselessness. I thought the snake thing wanted Lollo. It didn't. It dug its dagger into the roots of the bush which was of a dirty purplish color. As the dagger went in, the bush turned gray and all its

134

thorns went pale and soft. It died almost in_
the snake thing could go for Lollo.

But it was too slow, or too stupid: I just __ __
to grab her ankles and pull her away. I tow_ _ her
over to the muddy shore and flung her aboard
Flupper. I was yelling at Flupper to help, to do something, anything. But all he did was to leave the shore
and head fast for another part of the lagoon, where
the molds and fungi overhang the water. I begged
him not to, but he just went on, heading straight for
them.

"Home, take me home!" I shouted to Flupper. He
took no notice. I could say nothing to Lollo; she had become a silent, horrible, raw red thing. "Not this way!" I
shouted. "Home!"

But still Flupper continued in the wrong direction,
heading for the grayish clumps of mold and fungi. I
hated these growths, they frightened me. And Flupper
was not merely heading for them, he was among them!
"No!" I screamed. But it was too late: the sticky grayish
growths were brushing over Lollo's body, clinging to
her, damply caressing her, sticking to her in wisps and
clusters.

And Flupper had done this deliberately! I lay down
on him and beat him with my fists. I must have been
out of my mind . . .

Suddenly it didn't matter anymore. I lay there, head
buried in my arms, knowing that Lollo was dead: I
would spend the rest of my life cursing myself and
Flupper. Cursing and weeping.

Then Lollo's voice said, close to my ear, "Yuck! I am filthy! All *bloody!*"

I sat up and she was kneeling beside me, picking at herself disgustedly, trying to get rid of the fungi and molds. And—unbelievably—*as I watched, the cuts and stabs in her flesh healed.*

"All this *blood,*" she said, in just the same voice she'd have used if she'd spotted chocolate around my mouth. "How disgusting! You'll have to get it off. I can't."

Later, I helped her sponge off the caked blood. It took a long time, there was so much of it. We did it at home back at the unit. We never got rid of the stains on her gear. Those stains gave us away, of course. Dad spotted them and Mum tore us apart. A real tongue-lashing. Almost as bad as the thorn bush, Lollo said.

Our parents wouldn't believe a word we said, so we took them to see Flupper. Dad carried a Trans Vox so that we could talk properly with him. I'm amazed that Lollo and I never thought of using the Trans Vox: it translates almost any language into our language. Soon, everyone was talking away like mad.

A little later—just a few months—we were rich. Rich as you can get!

All thanks to Flupper, of course. And those growths that used to frighten me, the molds and the fungi.

You know about penicillin? Alexander Fleming discovered it quite early in the twentieth century. The wonder antibiotic, the great cure-all. Well, *our* molds and fungi (I mean, Flupper's) turned out to be super penicillin x 10,000. And Dad and Mum had staked the claim, so they have Galactic Rights.

So we were and are everlastingly rich. "Just think!" Mum said. "We can go back to our proper home! Live Earthside!"

"I don't want to go back home!" Lollo said. "I *won't* go, you can't *make* me go!"

Flupper, of course: she couldn't bear the thought of leaving him. I felt the same.

When we talked to Flupper about it, he said, "Do you know how old I am?" We said no. "I'm 245 Earth years old," he said. "And I've got another 150 to go . . ."

So perhaps Lollo and I won't make so much fuss about going back to Earth. We can always come back. And Flupper will always be there.

"Whooo-ooo, Flupper!"

THE DEAD PLANET

by Edmond Hamilton

It didn't look like such a forbidding little world at first. It looked dark, and lifeless, but there was no hint of what brooded there. The only question in our minds then was whether we would die when our crippled ship crashed on it.

Tharn was at the controls. All three of us had put on our pressure suits in the hope that they might save us if the crash was bad. In the massive metal suits we looked like three queer, fat robots, like three metal globes with jointed mechanical arms and legs.

"If it hadn't happened here!" came Dril's hopeless voice through the intercom. "Here in the most desolate and unknown part of the whole galaxy!"

"We're lucky we were within reaching distance of a star system when the generators let go," I murmured.

"Lucky, Oroc?" repeated Dril bitterly. "Lucky to postpone our end by a few days of agony? It's all we can look forward to on *that*."

The system ahead did look discouraging for wrecked star explorers. Here in a thin region at the very edge of the galaxy, it centered around a sun that was somber dark red, ancient, dying.

Six worlds circled that smoldering star. We were dropping toward the innermost of the six planets, as the most possibly habitable. But now, we could clearly see that life could not exist on it. It was an airless sphere, sheathed in eternal snow and ice.

The other five planets were even more hopeless. And we could not change course now, anyway. It was a question of whether the two strained generators that still functioned would be able to furnish enough power to slow down our landing speed and save us from total destruction.

Death was close, and we knew it, yet we remained unshaken. Not that we were heroes. But we belonged to the Star Service, and while the Star Service yields glory, its members always have the shadow of death over them and so grow accustomed to it.

Many in the Star Service had died in the vast, endless task of mapping the galaxy. Of the little exploring ships that went out like ours to chart the farther reaches of stars, only two-thirds or less ever came back. Accidents accounted for the rest—accidents like the blowing of our generators from overload in attempting to claw our way quickly out of a mass of interstellar debris.

Tharn's voice came to us calmly.

"We'll soon hit it. I'll try to crabtail in, but the chances are poor. Better strap in."

Using the metal arms of our suits clumsily, we hooked into the resilient harnesses that might give us a chance of survival.

Dril peered at the rapidly enlarging white globe below.

"There looks to be deep snow at places. It would be a little softer there."

"Yes," Tharn replied quietly. "But our ship would remain buried in the snow. On the ice, even if wrecked, it

141

could be seen. When another ship comes, they'll find us, and our charts won't be lost."

Well, for a moment that made me so proud of the Star Service that I was almost contemptuous of the danger rushing upon us.

It is that wonderful spirit that has made the Service what it is, that has enabled our race to push out from our little world to the farthest parts of the galaxy. Individual explorers might die, but the Service's conquest of the universe would go on.

"Here we go," muttered Dril, still peering downward.

The icy white face of the desolate world was rushing up at us with nightmare speed. I waited tensely for Tharn to act.

He delayed until the last moment. Then he moved the power bar, and the two remaining generators came on with a roar of power.

They could not stand that overload for more than a few moments before they too blew out. But it was enough for Tharn to swing the falling ship around and use the blast of propulsive vibrations as a brake.

Making a crabtail landing is more a matter of luck than skill. The mind isn't capable of estimating the infinitesimal differences that mean disaster or survival. Use a shade too much power, and you're bounced away from your goal. A shade too little, and you smash to bits.

Tharn was lucky. Or maybe it wasn't luck as much as pilot's instinct. Anyway, it was all over in a moment. The ship fell, the generators screamed, there was a bumping crash, then silence.

The ship lay on its side on the ice. Its stern had crumpled and split open at one place, and its air had puffed out, though in our suits we didn't mind that. Also the last two generators had blown out, as expected, from the overload in cushioning our fall.

"We've made it!" Dril bounded from despair to hope. "I never thought we had a real chance. Tharn, you're the ace of all pilots."

But Tharn himself seemed to suffer reaction from tension. He unstrapped like ourselves and stood, a bulky figure in his globular suit, looking out through the quartz portholes.

"We've saved our necks for the time being," he muttered. "But we're in a bad fix."

The truth of that sank in as we looked out with him. This little planet out on the edge of the galaxy was one of the most desolate I had ever seen. There was nothing but ice and darkness and cold.

The ice stretched in all directions, a rolling white plain. There was no air—the deep snows we had seen were frozen air, no doubt. Over the gelid plain brooded a dark sky, two-thirds of which was black emptiness. Across the lower third glittered the great drift of the galaxy stars, of which this system was a borderland outpost.

"Our generators are shot, and we haven't enough powerloy to wind new coils for all of them," Tharn pointed out. "We can't call a tenth the distance home with our little communicator. And our air will eventually run out.

"Our only chance," he continued decisively, "is to find on this planet enough tantalum and terbium and the other metals we need to make powerloy and wind new coils. Dril, get out the radiosonde."

The radiosonde was the instrument used in our star mapping to explore the metallic resources of unknown planets. It worked by projecting broad beams of vibrations that could be tuned to reflect from any desired elements, the ingenious device detecting and computing position thus.

Dril got out the compact instrument and tuned its frequencies to the half-dozen rare metals we needed. Then we waited while he swung the projector tubes along their quadrants, closely watching the indicators.

"This is incredible luck!" he exclaimed finally. "The sonde shows terbium, tantalum, and the other metals we need all together in appreciable quantities. They're just under the ice and not far from here!"

"It's almost too good to be true," I said wonderingly. "Those metals are never found all together."

Tharn planned quickly.

"We'll fix a rough sled, and on it we can haul an auxiliary power unit and the big dis-beam, to cut through the ice. We'll also have to take cables and tackle for a hoist."

We soon had everything ready and started across the ice, hauling our improvised sled and its heavy load of equipment.

The frozen world, brooding beneath the sky that looked out into the emptiness of extragalactic space, was oppressive. We had hit queer worlds before, but this was the most gloomy I had ever encountered.

The drift of stars that was our galaxy sank behind the horizon as we went on, and it grew even darker. Our krypton lamps cut a white path through the somber gloom as we stumbled on, the metal feet of our heavy suits slipping frequently on the ice.

Dril stopped frequently to make further checks with the radiosonde. Finally, after several hours of toilsome progress, he looked up from the instrument and made a quick signal.

"This is the position," he declared. "There should be deposits of the metals we need only thirty meters or so beneath us."

It didn't look encouraging. We were standing on the crest of a low hill of the ice, and it was not the sort of topography where you would expect to find a deposit of those metals.

But we did not argue with Dril's findings. We hauled the auxiliary power unit off the sledge, got its little auto-turbine going, and hooked its leads to the big dis-beam projector that we had dismounted from the bows of our ship.

Tharn played the dis-beam on the ice with expert skill. Rapidly, it cut a three-meter shaft down through the ice. It went down for thirty meters like a knife through cheese and then there was a sudden backlash of sparks and flame. He quickly cut the power.

"That must be the metal-bearing rock we just hit," he said.

Dril's voice was puzzled.

"It should be twenty-one to twenty-five meters lower to the metal deposits, by the sonde readings."

"We'll go down and see," Tharn declared. "Help me set up the winch."

We had brought heavy girders and soon had them formed into a massive tripod over the shaft. Strong cables

145

ran through pulleys suspended from that tripod and were fastened to a big metal bucket in which we could descend by paying out cable through the tackle.

Only two of us should have gone down, really. But somehow, none of us wanted to wait alone up on the dark ice, nor did any of us want to go down alone into the shaft. So we all three crowded into the big bucket.

"Acting like children instead of veteran star explorers," grunted Tharn. "I shall make a note for our psychos on the upsetting effect of conditions on these worlds at the galaxy edge."

"Did you bring your beam guns?" Dril asked suddenly.

We had, all of us. Yet we didn't know quite why. Some obscure apprehension had made us arm ourselves when there was no conceivable need of it.

"Let's go," said Tharn. "Hang onto the cable and help me pay it out, Oroc."

I did as he bade, and we started dropping smoothly down into the shaft in the ice. The only light was the krypton whose rays Dril directed downward.

We went down thirty meters, and then we all cried out. For we saw now the nature of the resistance which the dis-beam had met. Here under the ice there was thick stratum of transparent metal, and the dis-beam had had to burn its way through that.

Underneath the burned-out hole in that metal stratum there was—nothing. Just empty space, a great hollow of some kind here beneath the ice.

Tharn's voice throbbed with excitement.

"I'd already begun to suspect it. Look down there!"

The krypton beam, angling downward into the emptiness below us, revealed a spectacle that stunned us.

Here, beneath the ice, was a city. It was a great metropolis of white cement structures, dimly revealed by our little light. And this whole city was shielded by an immense dome of transparent metal that withstood the weight of the ice that ages had piled upon it.

"Our dis-beam cut down through the ice and then through the dome itself," Tharn was saying excitedly. "This dead city may have been lying hidden here for ages."

Dead city? Yes, it was dead. We could see no trace of movement in the dim streets as we dropped toward it.

The white avenues, the vague facades and galleries and spires of the metropolis, were silent and empty. There was no air here. There could be no inhabitants.

Our bucket bumped down onto the street. We fastened the cables and climbed out, stood staring numbly about us. Then we uttered simultaneous cries of astonishment.

An incredible thing was happening. Light was beginning to grow around us. Like the first rosy flush of dawn it came at first, burgeoning into a soft glow that bathed all the far-flung city.

"This place can't be dead!" exclaimed Dril. "That light—"

"Automatic trips could start the light going," said Tharn. "These people had a great science, great enough for that."

"I don't like it," Dril murmured. "I feel that the place is haunted."

I had that feeling, too. I am not ordinarily sensitive to alien influences. If you are, you don't get accepted by the Star Service.

But a dark, oppressive premonition such as I had never felt before now weighed upon my spirits. Deep in my consciousness stirred vague awareness of horror brooding in this silent city beneath the ice.

"We came here for metal, and we're going to get it," Tharn said determinedly. "The light won't hurt us, it will help us."

Dril set up the radiosonde and took bearings again. They showed strongest indications of the presence of the metals we needed at a point some halfway across the city from us.

There was a towering building there, an enormous pile whose spire almost touched the dome. We took it as our goal and started.

The metal soles of our pressure suits clanked on the smooth cement paving as we walked. We must have made a strange picture—we three in our grotesque metal armor tramping through that eerily illuminated metropolis of silence and death.

"This city is old indeed," Tharn said in a low voice. "You notice that the buildings have roofs? That means they're older than—"

"Tharn! Oroc!" yelled Dril suddenly, swerving around and grabbing for his beam pistol.

We saw it at the same moment. It was rushing toward us from a side street we had just passed.

I can't describe it. It was like no normal form of life. It was a gibbering monstrosity of black flesh that changed from one hideous shape to another with pro-tean rapidity as it *flowed* toward us.

The horror and hatred that assaulted our minds were

not needed to tell us that this thing was inimical. We fired our beams at it simultaneously.

The creature sucked back with unbelievable rapidity and disappeared in a flashing movement between two buildings. We ran forward. But it was gone.

"By all the devils of space!" swore Dril, his voice badly shaken. "What was *that?*"

Tharn seemed as stunned as we.

"I don't know. It was living, you saw that. And its swift retreat when we fired argues intelligence and volition."

"Ordinary flesh couldn't exist in this cold vacuum—" I began.

"There are perhaps more forms of life and flesh than we know," muttered Tharn. "Yet such things surely wouldn't build a city like this—"

"There's another!" I interrupted, pointing wildly.

The second of the black horrors advanced like a huge, unreared worm. But even as we raised our pistols, it darted away.

"We've got to go on," Tharn declared, though his own voice was a little unsteady. "The metals we need are in or near that big tower, and unless we get them we'll simply perish on the ice above."

"There may be worse deaths than freezing to death up there on the ice," said Dril huskily. But he came on with us.

Our progress through the shining streets of that magically beautiful white city was one of increasing horror.

The black monstrosities seemed to be swarming in the dead metropolis. We glimpsed and fired at dozens of them. Then we stopped beaming them, for we didn't seem able to hit them.

They didn't come to close quarters to attack us. They seemed rather to follow us and *watch* us, and their numbers and menacing appearance became more pronounced with every step we took toward the tower.

More daunting than the inexplicable creatures were the waves of horror and foreboding that were now crushing our spirits. I have spoken of the oppression we had felt since entering the city. It was becoming worse by the minute.

"We are definitely being subjected to psychological attack from some hostile source," muttered Tharn. "All this seems to be because we are approaching that tower."

"This system is on the edge of the galaxy," I reminded. "Some undreamed-of creature or creatures from the black outside could have come from there and laired up on this dead world."

I believe we would at that point have turned and retreated had not Tharn steadied us with a reminder.

"Whatever is here that is going to such lengths to force us to retreat is doing so because it's afraid of us! That argues that we can at least meet it on equal terms."

We were approaching the side flight of steps that led up to the vaulted entrance of the great tower. We moved by now in a kind of daze, crushed as we were by the terrific psychic attack that was rapidly conquering our courage.

Then came the climax. The lofty doors of the tower swung slowly open. And from within the building there lurched and shambled out a thing, the sight of which froze us where we stood.

"*That* never came from any part of our own galaxy!" Dril cried hoarsely.

It was black, mountainous in bulk and of a shape that tore the brain with horror. It was something like a monstrous, squatting toad, its flesh a heaving black slime from which protruded sticky black limbs that were not quite either tentacles or arms.

Its triangle of eyes were three slits of cold green fire that watched us with hypnotic intensity. Beneath that hideous chinless face its breathing pouch swelled in and out painfully as it lurched, slobbering, down the steps toward us.

Our beams lashed frantically at that looming horror. And they had not the slightest effect on it. It continued to lurch down the steps, and, most ghastly of all, there was in its outlines a subtly hideous suggestion that it was parent, somehow, to the smaller horrors that swarmed in the city behind us.

Dril uttered a cry and turned to flee, and I stumbled around to join him. But from Tharn came a sharp exclamation.

"Wait! Look at the thing! It's *breathing!*"

For a moment, we couldn't understand. And then, dimly, I did. The thing was obviously breathing. Yet there was no air here!

Tharn suddenly stepped forward. It was the bravest thing I have ever seen done by a member of the Star Service. He strode right toward the towering, slobbering horror.

And abruptly, as he reached it, the mountainous black obscenity vanished. It disappeared like a clicked-off televisor scene. And the black swarm in the city behind us disappeared at the same moment.

"Then it wasn't real?" Dril exclaimed.

"It was only a projected hypnotic illusion," Tharn declared. "Like the others we saw back there. The fact that it was breathing, here where there is no air, gave me the clue to its unreality."

"But then," I said slowly, "whatever projected those hypnotic attacks is inside this building."

"Yes, and so are the metals we want," Tharn said grimly. "We're going in."

The ceaseless waves of horror-charged thought beat upon us even more strongly as we went up the steps. Gibbering madness seemed to shriek in my brain as we opened the high doors.

And then, as we stepped into the vast, gleaming white nave of the building, all that oppressive mental assault suddenly ceased.

Our reeling minds were free of horror for the first time since we had entered this dead city. It was like bursting out of one of the great darkness clouds of the galaxy into clear space again.

"Listen!" said Tharn in a whisper. "I hear—"

I heard, too. We didn't really hear it, of course. It was not sound, but mental waves that brought the sensation of sound to our brains.

It was music we heard. Faint and distant at first, but swelling in a great crescendo of singing instruments and voices.

The music was alien, like none we had ever heard

before. But it gripped our minds as its triumphant strains rose and rose.

There were in those thunderous chords the titanic struggles and hopes and despairs of a race. It held us rigid and breathless as we listened to that supernal symphony of glory and defeat.

"They are coming," said Tharn in a low voice, looking across the white immensity of the great nave.

I saw them. Yet oddly I was not afraid now, though this was by far the strangest thing that had yet befallen us.

Out into the nave toward us was filing a long procession of moving figures. They were the people of this long-dead world, the people of the past.

They were not like ourselves, though they were bipedal, erect figures with a general resemblance to us in bodily structure. I cannot particularize them, they were so alien to our eyes.

As the music swelled to its final crescendo and then died away, the marching figures stopped a little away from us and looked at us. The foremost, apparently their leader, spoke, and his voice reached our minds.

"Whoever you are, you have nothing more to fear," he said. "There is no life in this city. All the creatures you have seen, all the horror that has attacked you, yes, even we ourselves who speak to you, are but phantoms of the mind projected from telepathic records that are set to start functioning automatically when anyone enters this city."

"I thought so," whispered Tharn. "They could be nothing else."

The leader of the aliens spoke on.

"We are a people who perished long ago, by your reckoning. We originated on this planet"—he called it by an almost unpronounceable alien name—"far back in your past. We rose to power and wisdom and then to glory. Our science bore us out to other worlds, to other stars, finally to exploration and colonization of most of the galaxy.

"But finally came disaster. From the abyss of extragalactic space came invaders so alien that they could never live in amity with us. It was inevitable war between us and them, we to hold our galaxy, they to conquer it.

"They were not creatures of matter. They were creatures made up of photons, particles of force—shifting clouds capable of unimaginable cooperation between themselves and of almost unlimited activities. They swept us from star after star, they destroyed us on a thousand worlds.

"We were finally hemmed in on this star system of our origin, our last citadel. Had there been hope for the future in the photon race, had they been creatures capable of creating a future civilization, we would have accepted defeat and destruction and would have abdicated thus in their favor. But their limitations of intelligence made that impossible. They would never rise to civilization themselves nor allow any other race in the galaxy to do so.

"So we determined that, before we perished, we would destroy them. They were creatures of force who could only be destroyed by force. We converted our sun into a gigantic generator, hurling some of our planets and moons into it to cause the cataclysm we desired. From our sun generator sprang a colossal wave of force that swept out and annihilated the photon race in one cosmic surge of energy.

"It annihilated the last of us also. But we had already prepared this buried city, and in it had gathered all that we knew of science and wisdom to be garnered by future ages. Some day new forms of life will rise to civilization in the galaxy, some day explorers from other stars will come here.

"If they are not intelligent enough to make benign use of the powers we have gathered here, our telepathic attacks should frighten them away. But if they are intelligent enough to discern the clues we leave for them, they will understand that all is but hypnotic illusion and will press forward into this tower of our secrets.

"You, who listen to me, have done this. To you, whoever and of whatever future race you may be, we bequeath our wisdom and our power. In this building, and in others throughout the city, you will find all that we have left. Use it wisely for the good of the galaxy and all its races. And now, from us of the past to you of the future—farewell."

The figures that stood before us vanished. And we three remained standing alone in the silent, shimmering white building.

"Space, what a race they must have been!" breathed Tharn. "To do all that, to die destroying a menace that would have blighted the galaxy forever, and still to contrive to leave all they had gained to the future!"

"Let's see if we can find the metals," begged Dril, his voice shaky. "All I want now is to get out of here and take a long drink of *sanqua*."

We found more than the metals we needed. In that wonderful storehouse of alien science, we found whole wave generators of a type far superior to ours, which could easily be installed in our crippled ship.

I shall not tell of all else we found. The Star Service is already carefully exploring that great treasury of ancient science, and in time its findings will be known to all the galaxy.

It took labor to get the generators back up to our ship, but when that was done, it was not hard to install them. And when we had fused a patch on our punctured hull, we were ready to depart.

As our ship arrowed up through the eternal dusk of that ice-clad world and darted past its smoldering dying sun on our homeward voyage, Dril took down the bottle of *sanqua.*

"Let's get these cursed suits off, and then I'm going to have the longest drink I ever took!" he vowed.

We divested ourselves of the heavy suits at last. It was a wonderful relief to step out of them, to unfold our cramped wings and smooth our ruffled feathers.

We looked at each other, we three tall bird-men of Rigel, as Dril handed us the glasses of pink *sanqua.* On Tharn's beaked face, in his green eyes, was an expression that told me we all were thinking of the same thing.

He raised the glass that he held in his talons.

"To that great dead race to whom our galaxy owes all," he said. "We will drink to their world by their own name for it. We will drink to Earth."

FUN ON PHROMINIUM

by Karen Jordan Allen

When the Earthers first came to Phrominium, my moms and dads told me to stay away from them. Yes, they said, our Elders *had* invited them to study our radio arrays. Yes, there were only twenty of them, and half were children like me. But they were Offworlders, and until we knew they were safe, we couldn't go near them.

Like every other child in town, though, I spent hours clinging to the fence around the Earther compound, watching the strange new people with fur only on their heads. And I knew that our parents would *never* consider them safe.

In the first place, their houses were tall, two or three times as tall as Phrome houses. With *steps*. That ruled out any visits from Phromes. We don't climb on steps or *anything*. "Climb knee high, fall and die," our parents always say.

And the clothes they wore! Red and yellow and green and blue and striped and spotted and patterned with flowers. Our tunics are the color of dirt and rocks and sponge-grass. Some of the older kids went to the compound gate and convinced the Earther kids to take their tunics in trade for Earther shirts. One of my cousins did that, and his parents made him stay in the house for a *month*, which is a lot longer on Phrominium than on Earth.

But besides all that, Earthers *fly*. Of course; they had to fly through space to get to Phrominium. Just the thought of having nothing under me makes me throw up. Phromes don't fly, but we have huge radio arrays; with them, we can listen to any place in the universe. That's how we found out about the Earthers, and why they came to live here.

I didn't meet any Earthers until Larina came to study with me under Arlhup the Mortician. Master Arlhup didn't like her, I could tell. He put his finger next to his nose and snorted three times, which adult Phromes are not supposed to do in front of children. And he smelled angry. But the Work Seer had sent Larina to Master Arlhup, and even a Master had to do what the Work Seer told him.

Master Arlhup gave Larina an apron and sent her to work with me arranging a Speaking Room. Dead Phromes are stuffed, dressed up, and put in a Speaking Room. All the relatives and friends have a turn sitting on a Speaking Pillow in front of the dead person, and talking to him. When the pillow is finished being used—and sometimes that doesn't happen for days—we put the stuffed Phrome outside the town wall, and the Gatherers take it away.

Anyway, it was Larina and me in the Speaking Room. She was almost as tall as an adult Phrome, with brown, hairless skin—except for her head, which was covered with black curls. I could tell right away why Arlhup didn't like her: she smelled funny—musty and sour and salty. But that wasn't her fault; people smell the way they smell.

159

I didn't know what to say since I had never seen an Earther close-up before. But Larina started talking. Her Phroman was better than I expected.

"I can't believe you don't have any schools!" she said. "Where do you learn to read and write? And did that Seer person send you here, too? I can't believe I have to work with *dead* people . . . though it's not like working with dead *humans*. At least you have that white fur all over your bodies, and I don't have to touch any cold, dead *skin*. What's your name, anyway? I'm Larina."

"Philorem," I said.

"Phuh-lor-um. How do you spell that? Are you a boy or a girl? I can't tell yet. You all dress alike—those awful, dull things. Would you like one of my brother's shirts? He has an orange one that's too small for him, but it might fit you."

"Yes, please," I said, wondering at the same time how to hide the garment from my parents. "I'm a boy. And you?"

"You can't tell, either? I'm a girl. I live with my brother and my mom and dad. You have lots of parents, don't you? That's weird. I do have friends who have stepmoms and dads, but they don't all *live* together."

My fur bristled a little. "I have six parents: three mothers and three fathers. And eight brothers and sisters. One of our parents teaches us at home until we are old enough for the Work Seer to assign us an apprenticeship."

Larina nodded. She didn't seem to notice the smell of my annoyance. You can always tell what Phromes are feeling by how we smell.

"How do the Work Seers know where to send you?" Larina asked. "All she did was put her hands on my head and then tell my parents I was supposed to be a mortician. Did she *know?* Or was she just making it up?"

"Work Seers *never* make things up." I was beginning to wish that Arlhup had put Larina to work with someone else. No one *ever* questioned the Work Seers. "They know from the way we smell and the way our brains vibrate."

"But how can they tell with Earthers? Maybe our brains don't vibrate the same. We're not acrophobic like you are. That's what my dad says," she added. "That means you're afraid of heights."

"What's the matter with that?" I asked. My anger smelled so strong and bitter that my nose twitched. "Falls can kill you."

"So can lots of things. Is that why your houses are all so flat?"

Before I could answer, Master Arlhup looked in from the doorway. "You haven't done a thing, and the relatives are waiting at the front door! Show her the cushions, Philorem. Bring in the flowers! Start the incense! Move, move, move!"

Larina looked at me and rolled her eyes, but I just motioned for her to follow me to the cushion room.

"What's his problem?" she whispered when Master Arlhup was out of sight. "Is he always like this?"

I nodded as I pawed through the Speaking Pillows. We needed an extra-large, tough pillow; the dead woman to be placed in that room had many relatives, and some of them had eaten too much.

"And I have to study with *him?*" Larina said. "For *years?*"

"Just two years," I said, wondering if all Earthers were so whiny.

"But that's almost *six* Earth years. How do you stand it? Well, my dad may transfer out before then. He didn't want to come here, but he had to, because radio equipment is his specialty. My mom is an exozoologist—that means she studies animals on other planets. She's really interested in those Gatherer things. What do they do, anyway? They're bigger than you are, and so *ugly!* They remind me of our gorillas, except for their green faces. Aren't you afraid of them? They're everywhere."

I found a large, green Speaking Pillow and set it aside. "Find the small pillows that match this one," I told Larina. They would be for the mourners waiting their turn.

She dug into the pile. "So? The Gatherers? What are they?"

"The Gatherers gather things," I said. "And they serve us by taking away the things we don't need."

"Like garbage collectors? Where do they take everything? We finally started storing our garbage on other planets when we ran out of room."

Flying to other planets just to store garbage? I shuddered. "We think they take most of it to the mountains. We never go there. But sometimes we find Gatherer piles in the plains outside town. They sort everything.

Foot coverings here, old floor sweepers there, a mound of dead pincher-ants over there."

"Pincher-ants! I hate them! They're as big as my *hand*." Larina shivered. "Do the Gatherers ever take anything they're not supposed to?"

"Mmm. Well, once everyone was missing their pots for making sportleleaf tea. We found them all in a pile outside the wall. But we feed the Gatherers and never, ever hurt them, so they usually serve us well."

"Some of them even come into the compound. Guess I'd better not leave anything in the yard, huh? Here— are these the pillows you want?"

Fortunately, Larina could work almost as fast as she could talk. The Speaking Room was ready by the time Master Arlhup returned, so he didn't make us go work with the taxidermists, which was his favorite punishment for lazy apprentices.

Somehow I always ended up working with Larina after that, but she did bring me the orange shirt, so I didn't mind. Master Arlhup would hardly even look at her, just wave her in my direction. "Earthers! They should never have come! Whiny, arrogant Offworlders! We'd be well rid of them."

I hoped Larina didn't hear. She annoyed me sometimes, but she was always cheerful and said what she thought, and I liked that.

Then one day, Larina arrived wild-eyed and smelling scared.

"Master Arlhup! Master Arlhup!" she exclaimed. "Help us! They're all gone! Our parents are gone!"

Master Arlhup looked her up and down. "Whose parents?"

"*Ours.* The *Earthers.* All the grown-ups. I got up for breakfast and they were gone!"

He turned away with a shrug. "Probably killed themselves falling off of something. Shouldn't be climbing on steps. Shouldn't be living in houses one on top of the other. Shouldn't be flying around in space."

"Don't you care? Aren't you going to help me?"

I winced, and Master Arlhup covered his ears. The noises coming from her mouth were deafening.

"Larina! You have work to do!" said Master Arlhup.

"I can't work, I have to talk to someone. Don't you have any police? Somebody?"

Master Arlhup stepped in front of the door. "Listen to me. Your brother isn't gone, is he?"

Larina shook her head.

"The other children aren't gone, are they?"

She shook her head again.

"Your parents wouldn't leave you, would they?"

She stared at the floor.

"Then what's to worry about? Like as not they'll be home tonight. Now don't bother me. Philorem, keep her busy."

"Yes, sir." But I could smell how frightened she was. She hardly spoke all day, too, and that made me nervous. I didn't know what Earthers did to comfort each other. So I didn't do anything. Except I told her, "If they're still gone tomorrow, I'll help you."

"Thanks," she muttered. "Nobody else cares."

"If they're *really* gone, the Elders will want to know," I said. "You must have Elders, too, somewhere?"

"We have people in charge, but we don't call them Elders. My dad has to make reports. If he doesn't get his reports in, someone will come looking for him."

"There. So don't worry."

I must have said the wrong thing, because she started to cry. I got busy putting some cushions away, and when she did talk to me again she asked how long before we had a food break.

Before she left, I told her again I'd help her if her parents were still missing.

But the next day, *she* didn't show up, either.

"Good riddance," said Master Arlhup, when I asked him about Larina. "She would have been unreliable. Can't trust Offworlders."

"But she learned very fast, sir." I didn't think he was being fair.

"Fast work breeds errors," he said. "Get busy."

But I couldn't stop thinking about Larina. That evening, before I went home, I went to the Earthers' compound. The gate was open, and the buildings were frighteningly quiet. I smelled terrified Earthers and something else. Something familiar.

Gatherers.

The Gatherers had been here. Lots of them.

Had they gathered up the Earthers?

I ran home and told my parents what I thought had

happened. They shook their heads and looked worried, but didn't have any suggestions.

"With Offworlders, who knows what they're doing?" my dad Harnium said. "Maybe they went somewhere. Or they left. We shouldn't expect to understand them. Now drink up your soup."

But I knew Larina, and I didn't think she would just leave without saying good-bye.

I had to do something.

The next morning, I didn't go to Master Arlhup's. Instead, I went back to the Earthers' compound and sniffed around until I found Larina's house. Then I followed her scent across the compound and through the gate.

The trail led around the edge of town and straight across the Empty Green Plains to the mountains.

We have no name for the mountains. They are not far—a morning's walk, no more—but we do not go there. They are too frightening, too high. We would rather die than climb them, so we leave them to the Gatherers.

But where else would they take the Earthers?

I went back inside the wall long enough to buy a flask of water and some fried pincher-ant eggs, and then set off across the plain alone.

The sun seemed hotter here than in town, and I pulled the loose neck of my tunic up over my head to shade my face. It blocked my view of the mountains, but I didn't need to look where I was going. I just followed

Larina's scent trail through the sponge-grass. There were several other scents, both Earther and Gatherer, but I concentrated on Larina's.

Sooner than I liked, I reached the rocky base of a cliff. The trail went around a pile of old tunics left by the Gatherers, and then went up through the rocks.

I would have to climb.

I stepped up on a rock, but it made me so dizzy I had to go down on my hands and knees to crawl. My stomach hurt.

Knee high, fall and die, I thought.

I looked up at the mountain. Big mistake.

Mountaintop, scream and drop.

I pulled up the neck of my tunic until all I could see was the rock path right in front of me, and I crawled up the mountain, sniffing Larina's trail.

The higher I went, the more my stomach hurt, and I threw up three times. Then my head ached until I thought my skull would split. My hands started to bleed, so I took off my foot coverings and put them on like gloves.

But I still smelled Larina, frightened and desperate. I couldn't give up.

Once I stopped to sip a little water and peeked back toward the town. The sight astounded me—the vast, yellow-walled city, the flat roofs of our houses, the long rows of silver squares that made up our radio array. How *big* it all was. Down in the middle of it all, it did not seem so big.

Then the sky suddenly whirled and I covered my

face so I wouldn't throw up the water I had just drunk.

The trail soon led me over a ridge, putting the town out of sight. Down I went, and that was worse than going up, with the weight of my body pulling me toward the bottom. I went on my stomach when the trail was steep. What if I fell? Or slid? No Phrome would ever find me here.

Finally I reached the bottom, where a tiny stream snaked through the valley. I stood up and crossed. The scent of Earthers was very strong now, and seemed to be in the breeze, not just on the rock.

"Growr!"

I jumped back as a huge Gatherer leaped down in front of me. He bared his large, flat teeth and shook his fists. The whiskers on his head twitched.

I had never heard one growl before. Or smell so dangerous. Before I could think what to say, he grabbed me, threw me over his shoulder, and climbed swiftly through the rocks. I closed my eyes. I knew I was going to die.

Then I heard voices—angry voices. The smell of frightened Earthers nearly drowned me. The Gatherer put me down and pushed me forward. I opened my eyes and stumbled into the arms of a large Earther man. Behind him stood the other Offworlders.

"A Phrome! I thought they didn't climb mountains!" he said. "I wonder what else they've lied about."

"Shh, he's just a boy. The Gatherer must have brought him," said a softer voice.

Someone shook my shoulder. "What's going on? Why have the Gatherers brought us here?"

"They won't let us out," another said. "We need food and water. Tell them to let us go."

I covered my ears. My legs buckled and I fell to the ground.

"Let me see him! Get out of the way, he's my friend!" Larina's voice cut through the mutterings. I sat up. She knelt beside me.

"Philorem? Whatever are you doing here? I thought you didn't climb mountains. Or did the Gatherer bring you here?"

"I climbed. Most of the way." I shuddered at the memory. "It made me sick. But I was worried."

She leaned forward and lowered her voice. "I don't know what's going on. The Gatherers brought us here. They've surrounded us and won't let us go. We're really hungry, and they'll only bring us water a cup at a time. Can you tell them to let us go?"

"I'll try," I said. But I hadn't had much practice commanding Gatherers. That was an adult job.

I stood up straight and looked around. Rock rose high on all sides, and Gatherers sat or stood on ledges looking down at us. The Gatherer who had carried me in guarded a narrow passage through the rock.

"Let us go, Gatherer!" I said in what I hoped was a commanding voice.

It didn't move. I wondered if it even heard me.

"I am Philorem, son of Kadesha, Rorka, Findelp, Halborin, Fidusha, and Harnium. In the name of my parents, let us pass."

The Gatherer stared in the other direction.

I thought of Larina standing behind me and tried one more time. "I am Philorem, apprentice of Master Arlhup the Mortician. In his name, I command you to stand aside."

The Gatherer raised his arms and stared, as they do when surprised.

Encouraged, I tried again. "Master Arlhup sent me. You must let us go!"

He motioned to the other Gatherers. They leaped from their perches and ran to us. Whiskers quivering, they sniffed me over. I hoped I still had a little of the mortuary's scent on me.

The Gatherers looked at me, sniffed some more, looked at the Earthers, and grunted and flapped their arms. Finally they filed out through the passage in the rock and left us alone.

Someone shouted. A man rushed past me. "I'll go first," he said. He returned in a few minutes. He said something in Earther language, and then to me in Phroman, "No Gatherers anywhere! Let's get out of here!"

The Earthers left their rocky prison faster than a herd of quifflips. A few of them patted my head or my shoulders as they went by. "Thank you," they said.

Larina grabbed my hand and pulled me toward the opening.

"No, no!" I said. "I can't go that fast. I'll be ill! *Knee high, fall and die. Mountaintop, scream and drop!*"

"Well, I can't just leave you here alone. Come on."

I clung to her as she dragged me up the mountain

and down, and I hoped I wouldn't throw up on her. I *almost* made it. Luckily, my stomach was pretty empty, and Larina seemed more worried about me than her foot coverings.

When we reached the town, the Earthers went right to the house of the head Elder and demanded to talk. I didn't hear what they said, but several things did happen afterwards.

First of all, the Elders learned that Master Arlhup had commanded the Gatherers to take the Earthers. So the Elders took Master Arlhup from his mortuary and put him to work picking sportleleaves.

Second, both the Earthers and the Phromes decided that we should get to know each other better. So the Earthers moved out of the compound and into Phrome houses. Larina's family moved in next to mine, and my parents discovered they liked her mom and dad quite a lot. They taught us to play checkers. We taught them spidflip.

Finally, all of Master Arlhup's apprentices had to go back to the Work Seer for new assignments. Larina and I went together.

The Work Seer sat on a pillow in a tiny, stuffy room, with a boy Phrome next to her to write down the assignments. I sat down in front of her. A dark veil covered all of her except her hands, which she put on my head. Her twelve fingers dug into my skull. She hummed. She fell silent.

"How odd," she said. She pointed at Larina. "You. Earther girl. Sit down."

Larina squeezed onto the pillow next to me. The Work Seer put one hand on her head and one on mine. She hummed. Stopped. Hummed. Stopped.

"No, don't wiggle," she said. "Mmmmmm . . ."

I held my breath. This had never happened before. A Work Seer *never* hesitated.

"Master Philorem and Master Larina," she said at last. "You will start a hiking school. Teach Phrome children to climb."

The Work Seer's hands dropped. Then she waved at the Phrome girl waiting behind Larina and me. "Come back later. I have a headache."

I looked at Larina. Her eyes were wide, and she smelled surprised—almost as surprised as I did. Teach *climbing?* With an *Earther?* To *Phrome* children? What would my parents say? What would the *other* children's parents say?

Then Larina's smell changed. She was annoyed— *really* annoyed. She jumped to her feet, nearly knocking me off the pillow, and stood, putting her fists on her hips.

"I don't believe this," she said. "I have to climb?" She waved a hand at me. "With *him?* He'll throw up on me!"

My head-fur bristled. "It was *your* fault for going so fast I couldn't crawl!" I shot back. "You didn't have to drag me off the mountain!"

"I couldn't just leave you there, could I?" Larina said with a sneer. "We'd still be waiting for you to climb down!" She turned to the Work Seer. "You see? *How* am

I supposed to teach climbing with somebody who's afraid to even walk up steps?"

The Work Seer sighed.

"Oh?" I said. "Well, maybe *I* don't want to work with *you*, either."

The Work Seer shook her head and held up both hands. She smelled even more annoyed than Larina.

"Take the work, don't shirk," said the Seer.

Larina frowned. "But I don't know anything about running a school. He doesn't, either. And who would come? Phromes don't climb."

I froze. *No one* ever talked back to a Work Seer. Not even grown-ups.

But the Seer just sighed again. "Oh, my head," she whispered. Then she leaned toward us, so close I could see her eyes through the veil. "Work Seers never give impossible tasks," she said firmly.

For once, even Larina had the sense not to answer back. The Seer stood up and left through a dark, curtained doorway. Her assistant followed.

Larina looked down at me. "Do we have to do what she says?"

I nodded. "No one ever disobeys a Work Seer."

"Oh." Larina slowly sank back down on the pillow and just sat there, quiet, for a whole minute.

I began to worry. "I won't throw up on you next time," I said. "I promise. You can go ahead of me."

"It's okay," Larina said. She shrugged. "You couldn't help it. Anyway, you probably saved all our lives. So, if teaching your friends how to climb is a way for me to start paying back that debt . . ." Then she smiled. "Besides, *anything's* better than working for Master Arlhup. And who knows? It might be fun."

Fun?

I thought about how sick I'd felt, crawling up and down the mountain. Then I remembered how I'd thrown up on Larina when she was helping me back down.

But then I remembered the magnificent view from the top.

Maybe Larina was right. Maybe it *could* be fun.

Larina stood up and held out her hand. I let her pull me up from the pillow, and we left the Work Seer's house. All our parents were waiting outside.

"What did she say?" they wanted to know.

"You're not going to believe this," Larina said.

I grinned. "No, you're not. But it's going to be fun. Lots of fun!"

SWEET HOME

by Nancy Varian Berberick

Irdha kicked the stuffed blue gimelatt across the little cabin.

"Stupid!" she shouted. "Stupid, stupid, *stupid!*" The gimelatt's six arms and four legs went spinning wildly, its three green eyes seemed shocked by the violence.

Davy, Irdha's brother, snorted and said, "You'd never do that to a real gim and get away with it."

Irdha stuck out her tongue, feeling foolish and no better for having done it.

"Aw, c'mon, Irdha, grow up, will you? You've been pouting for weeks and everyone's getting tired of it." But even as he said that, Davy turned away to peer out the big, oval PlexiClear window at all the stars and the never-ending night of space. Davy was thirteen, three years older than Irdha, but the way he acted sometimes you'd think he was as old as a grandfather.

He's stupid, too, Irdha decided as she scooped up the toy gimelatt and hugged it to her. You'd never do that to a real gimelatt and get away with it, either.

Irdha's eyes misted with tears. "Davy, I'll never see a real gimelatt again, not ever." That was probably true, but it wasn't the reason Irdha wanted to cry. Not the real reason.

Oh, Mom, I miss you so much!

Davy, still watching the starfield, muttered something about how she'd only ever seen a real gim once at the zoo and then she was scared of all the tusks and teeth. "You went screaming to Mom and. . . ."

His voice got gruff and tight and then his words trailed off. That always happened when he spoke of Mom. It happened to Dad, too, and often Irdha saw tears in Dad's eyes. Little by little, she'd stopped talking to them about Mom. It only made them get more gruff and even quieter.

Oh, Mom, if only I could talk to you. . . .

But, of course, if Mom were here Irdha wouldn't need to talk about the terrible empty sadness that lived inside her now.

Outside the window, stars hung like diamonds, winking and shining. Out there, in the dark and the stars, lay Bifrost, her homeworld. Tears pricked painfully. There was Mom, too, buried in the small, neat cemetery beside Thunder Falls where the water fell in a rush and roar and cast up plumes of spray, breathtaking sweeps of diamonds against the lemony yellow sky.

The quiet throb of the *Sojourner*'s engines made a rhythm, that rhythm woke up a ghost.

> Spinning, spinning, our ship is spinning!
> Turning like a wheel, weaving paths.
> In and out we go, back and forth,
> Out and in we sail, forth and back.
>
> Spinning, spinning, our ship is spinning
> Down the sky, around the stars.
> Threads and paths and trails we wind
> Spinning down all the roads to home.

177

Mom used to sing that song in a low, sweet voice as she tucked in Davy and Irdha and kissed them off to sleep. And she'd say, "One day we'll all go spinning home. We'll all go spinning down the sky, leaving home to go home."

Mom used to talk like that. She had been a poet, and poets have strange and beautiful ideas, or so Dad always said. Mom had longed to return to Earth ever since Irdha was born, and so great was her longing that she'd named Irdha after a goddess from an ancient story whose name means "Earth." But Mom had died of Terillian Fever before she had the chance to return to the planet where she'd been born.

Mom! Oh, Mom, I miss you. . . .

Irdha blinked away tears. Mom had died three months before, but it seemed to Irdha that each time she thought of her mother it was like hearing the terrible news of her death all over again. And now she was leaving Bifrost—leaving Mom!—because Dad said he couldn't bear to live there anymore. He said he had to leave home to go home.

Irdha smoothed the toy gim's soft blue plush. "You can't leave home to go home. It makes no sense."

"Makes sense to everyone but you," Davy said.

Irdha didn't argue, for it was true. Everyone seemed to think this was a good idea. Just pack up and go back to Earth. Dad already had a job there, Davy and Irdha were already enrolled in school. They'd live with Great-aunt Iowen until Dad could find a house for them. It was all settled within two months of Mom's death. All settled, and they were going to Earth. All settled, and they were leaving Mom behind, buried by Thunder Falls and so far, far away even now.

Irdha hugged the gim harder. Maybe everyone else thought it was settled, but she didn't. A chill made up of determination—and a little bit of fear—spidered along her neck. No matter what everyone else said, she just wasn't going to go and that's all there was to it.

Well, not all there was to it. There was the matter of her being on board the ship and two days on the journey already. . . .

Irdha tucked the blue gim under her arm and left the cabin. She had an idea, but to make it work she had to talk to her cousin Siubhan who was now tens of thousands of miles away.

Sojourner was a commercial transport run by a corporation that had offices on Bifrost and Earth and dozens of other planets in between. On this leg of the Bifrost-to-Earth run her hold was full of trade goods from Bifrost that would be sold for a large profit on Earth—Fairy Hens with their jewel-like eyes and gossamer plumage, singing crystals, steelwood and the like.

The cabin Irdha shared with Davy and her father was a small one, just enough room for a pair of bunk beds on either side of the room, one desk and a tiny bathroom. She settled into the chair at the desk and tapped the blue button at the right-hand corner. A 3DVid screen whooshed up from under the desktop. She knew, because she'd checked, that *Sojourner* was still within calling range of Bifrost. With quick fingers she tapped in the calling code and the 3DVid jumped into life showing Irdha her cousin's surprised face.

"Ird! What's up? Why are you calling—is something wrong?"

"No—yes—oh, Siubhan, I need your help! I can't go. I can't go and stay on Earth. I have to come home and I think I know how."

Siubhan's blue eyes lighted at the idea of Irdha's return, and just as suddenly she looked doubtful, gnawing on her bottom lip as she always did when troubled. "Ird, I don't know. . . ."

"Yeah, but I *do* know. Listen: you know how your parents and mine always let us spend holidays together, at my house or yours?"

Siubhan nodded, still gnawing.

"Well, why don't we just remind them of that and ask if—"

Siubhan's mind leapt ahead. "Ask if you can live with us?"

"It could be done," Irdha said. "I mean, I'd probably have to go back to Earth for the holidays, maybe even for school breaks, but kids do that all the time. Remember those twins in our class last year? The ones who were shuttling back and forth between Bifrost and their mom's homeworld so they could spend time with their grandparents . . . ?"

Siubhan stopped gnawing and started smiling. "Your dad used to say he envied those kids, traveling between two worlds all the time. He said they were getting great educations in both cultures, the one on Bifrost and the one on their mom's home planet."

Irdha hadn't remembered that, but now her heart felt light as Fairy Hen feathers. This could work!

But for the plan to work, they'd have to be fast about getting permission. Tomorrow, *Sojourner* would be at Boost Point Nine, one of those strange hiccups in space that would catapult them across uncounted miles. Within a moment of being Boosted, they'd be only a day's journey from Earth's solar system.

"Siubhan, hurry and go talk to your folks, and I'll talk to my dad. I'll call you back when I know."

Irdha broke the connection and thumbed another button on the desk. Now a soft voice asked: *What story would you like to hear?* Irdha's eyes stung with tears. That was Mom's voice, programmed into the computer a few years ago when the mechanical voice had frightened Irdha.

"Mom," she whispered, just as she used to when she was a little girl. "Tell me about our vacation in the desert."

With a muted chime, the program complied, replacing the last image of Siubhan with one of blue-green tors rising from a desert floor like stone fists thrusting up. In the yellow sky, pink clouds sailed before the wind. Above the horizon, three of Bifrost's nine moons were just rising, tiny and golden. On the desert floor, sand turned red and yellow and blue under the moonlight. Long ago, the desert at moon-rise had reminded the original colonists of the shining rainbow bridge of ancient Earth legends. That bridge, the old stories said,

181

would take you right to the magical land where gods live.

Irdha leaned closer, then sighed to see four small figures walking 'round the base of the tallest tor. These images were of Mom and Dad and Irdha and Davy, two years ago when everyone was well and everyone was happy. The image of her mother looked up at the sky and pointed to something, perhaps a leatherwing sailing by. She laughed and touched Dad's arm to draw his attention to what she saw. Irdha reached into the three-dimensional picture, trying to touch her mother. The image scattered all over her hand and disappointment choked her. That's all she'd ever have of her mother now, images too thin to touch. But if she went home, if she could go back to Bifrost . . . what would she have?

She'd have all the places Mom used to be, the paths she walked on in the garden outside their house, the blue-green road winding all the way to school where Mom used to walk every day on her way to work in the library complex. She'd have the air Mom breathed, the sky that used to look down on her. She'd have the little grave by Thunder Falls where she could go and plant flowers and talk to her mother. Bifrost would be her own rainbow bridge.

A moment later, the 3DVid program beeped, telling Irdha she had an in-coming call. Irdha froze the image on her desk and it dropped into the background. Now she saw her cousin's face shining with happiness. Siubhan's parents had agreed to talk to Irdha's father about the girls' idea, saying they'd be glad to have their niece come and stay with them for as long as her father thought best.

Irdha grinned. She signed off and the image of her mother came back into the foreground of her desk.

"Oh, Mom," Irdha whispered. "Mom, I'll be home soon. . . ."

Dad wore his frown like a storm. Irdha heard his stern "No," before he even spoke it. Davy sat across the cabin, perched on Irdha's bunk. He shook his head and glanced at Dad as if to say, "When will she grow up?"

"Irdha," Dad said, using that tone Irdha knew so well, the one that told her she'd get no chance to argue. "This is by far the most foolish scheme I've ever heard!"

"But, Dad—"

"No 'buts,' Irdha. You can put this idea right out of your mind. I thought we got this all straight before we left: you're coming with Davy and me to Earth. There will be no question about it."

No matter how hard she bit them, Irdha's lips began to quiver. Dad saw this and sighed. He reached across the table to take Irdha's hand. "What's gotten into you, Irdha? I can't imagine why you think I'd agree to such a crazy idea."

"Dad—I miss Mom! I don't want to leave her! Dad, please!"

Davy looked away, Dad lowered his eyes. Stubbornly, Irdha went on anyway.

"No one ever asked me whether I wanted to leave home. No one ever asked me what I wanted to do." The silence in the room became deeper and more uncomfortable. This was the point where she should have sighed and walked away, giving up. But Irdha took a big deep breath and went on anyway. "I don't want to leave home! I don't want to go to Earth! I want to stay with Mom."

Dad got up and walked around the little cabin. Davy turned and looked out the window. No one said anything. Irdha kept still for a long time, her eyes on the desktop where only moments before an image of her mother had stood, laughing and pointing to the sky. She shivered, feeling suddenly cold and alone. Trying one last time, she looked up and said, "I thought you'd agree to my idea because you love me and you care about me."

Dad's expression softened. "But, Irdha, it's because I love you that I want you to be with us. Don't you understand?"

"No," Irdha said, and it was hard to talk because her throat was closing up tight. "All I understand is that you're being so selfish! You want to go to Earth because you think you can't stay on Bifrost without Mom. You think things will be better because once Earth was your home. But it's not *my* home! My home is Bifrost—my home is where Mom is!"

"But, sweetheart—"

Irdha's tears burst from her. It seemed like her heart was being torn from her body. Her plan had failed! She jumped up and ran from the cabin, crying as hard as she'd ever cried in her life.

*   *   *

In the middle of the next night, *Sojourner* hit the Boost Point and leapt so smoothly across thousands of space-miles that Irdha never felt it. When she woke in the morning, they were a day away from Earth.

Now, she and Davy started gathering up clothing and toys to pack them away. Dad went around after them, finding socks behind the bunks and 3DVid data tubes under the tables. His mood was happier than Irdha had seen in weeks. Once he snatched up a bright pink nightgown from the floor by Irdha's bed.

"Pack it up, pack it up." He winked and smiled. "You wouldn't want to suddenly find out you'd left behind your sleeping gear after the ship leaves the dock."

Feeling sullen and resentful, Irdha grumbled that he knew very well the ship wasn't going anywhere for at least a day after it put down on Earth. The crew had to unload the trade goods.

"We could come and get anything we leave behind," she muttered.

Dad patted her cheek kindly, and Irdha shoved the nightgown into her case. She looked around her and found nothing more to pack. The blue stuffed gimelatt lay on her bunk and she picked it up and stood by the window, watching the stars go by as they came closer and closer to a <u>world</u> she had never seen, an alien world she never wanted to see.

Irdha stood holding her breath at *Sojourner*'s open hatchway, hugging the gimelatt hard to her chest. A ramp sloped gently down to a white paved area where a swirl of people embraced Davy and Dad. Their voices rose in joyful cries of welcome, the laughter of travelers returned at last, the glad cries of those who had waited so long to greet them. Irdha hung back, keeping near *Sojourner*'s doorway.

In the hard blue sky, small black creatures flew. They sailed the sky like the leatherwings of home, but they were so small, and they flew so high, that Irdha couldn't see if the resemblance ended there. On the ground, Davy pointed to the little flying creatures and shouted, "Birds!" with great delight in his voice. Davy was home, and happy to be. Irdha shivered miserably, feeling like an orphan.

Above the little birds, white puffy clouds ran boldly before a brisk wind. Irdha had to shade her eyes when she looked up at them. They were so bright! With a pang, she remembered the pink and lavender clouds of home. Beyond the landing area, the ground of Earth stretched out in wide, hilly sweeps, fields of some kind of vegetation bending before the wind. There seemed to be nothing on the whole of Earth but this green waving sea with a strange blue sky stretching over all.

Then, when she turned and looked in another direction, Irdha saw the dark, squat shape of one lonely little house crouching on the edge of the fields about a mile away. That was Great-aunt Iowen's house, and all around it the waving green was her farm. The green, Dad had said, was wheat and it would soon ripen to gold. Then all that gold would be harvested and made into food for people to eat.

"Irdha!" Dad called, waving from the paved ground. "Come down, Irdha, and meet your family!"

Irdha took a deep breath and started down the ramp.

"Irdha!" cried an old man just before he embraced her.

"Irdha!" laughed a little boy who tugged on her left hand even as a small girl tugged on her right arm.

The blue gimelatt fell to the ground. Irdha bent to snatch it up, but all the people crowding close swept it out of reach, tumbling it away like a ball till Irdha couldn't see it anymore.

Irdha! Irdha! Irdha!

They all seemed to know her, they all seemed to have been waiting for her, and the sound of their voices calling her name was the sound of a party getting under way. A party to which she did not want to go. She looked around for the gim and couldn't find it. Dad picked her up in his arms and held her against his shoulder as he carried her out of the crowd.

On the edge of the gathering, a tall old woman with twinkling blue eyes put a hand on Dad's arm to stop him for a moment, but she didn't try to say anything, or even touch Irdha. She only held up the blue gim and gave it to Irdha to hug.

"Thank you," Irdha whispered.

"I'm your Great-aunt Iowen," the woman said. "Welcome home, child."

She offered her hand and timidly Irdha took it. But then Great-aunt Iowen smiled and Irdha turned quickly away. That smile was Mom's smile, wide and bright and perfect. It went like an arrow to Irdha's heart, opening up all the wounds of pain and loss again.

This was not home! No matter who welcomed her, no matter what anyone said, this was not home! Irdha looked over her father's shoulder, past the crowd, to the dark bulk of *Sojourner* rising on the landing field. Hope sprang in her suddenly, like a light turned on.

She *would* get home, she would. And she knew what she had to do to get there.

Irdha stood still as stone at her bedroom door. At her feet sat a pillowcase stuffed with clothing. She hugged the blue gimelatt tightly under her arm. She held her breath to listen. No sound came but the little creaks Great-aunt Iowen's house made.

"Never let it worry you, child," she'd said, laughing, when she poked her head in the door to say good night. "This old house has been talking to itself for years and years." Then she'd winked and smiled—Mom's smile!—and whispered, "Good night, little Irdha, and welcome home."

I'm not home, Irdha had muttered, but not aloud, only in her mind. *But I will be soon. . . .*

I will *be*, she thought now, standing by the door. She heard Dad snoring in the room across the hall. She heard Davy sighing in his sleep in the room next to hers. She didn't hear Great-aunt Iowen, but her room was far down the long hallway. On bare silent feet Irdha stepped out into the hall. She looked right and then left. Nothing moved. She picked up her sack and tiptoed down the hall toward the big wide kitchen where they'd all eaten supper. Now and then the floor squeaked and creaked under her but she didn't stop, hoping that if anyone heard they would think of what Great-aunt Iowen said about the house talking to itself.

Irdha padded through the kitchen to the back door. Outside the wind whistled low around the eaves of the house. She waited till it gusted so the noise would cover any sound she'd make opening the back door, then stepped outside into the yard. She'd heard from Dad and Davy that Earth had only one white moon, and there it hung, thin as a finger nail. How strange and lonely it seemed with no other moons to keep it company!

Nothing moved but a thousand stars glittering above, and the wind running through the green wheat. Irdha knew where to go—she'd been careful to watch how they'd come here from the landing area. She would have to travel far down the winding road before she got to *Sojourner*, but she was sure she'd get there before anyone knew she was gone. Then it was simply a matter of being careful for a little while, and then clever enough to sneak on-board while the crew was still unloading portions of the cargo. If she kept still and quiet enough in some far corner of the ship no one would know she was there till it was too late to turn back.

"Then they'll *have* to take us back to Bifrost," she whispered to the blue gim. And that way Dad would see that this idea of bringing them all to live on Earth was wrong. He'd finally understand that Irdha needed to be home.

189

Beneath the stars, with the wind at her back, Irdha started down the road. She slipped past the house and snuck through the shadows thrown by the hay barns and the tractor sheds. Once free of the shadows and on the road, she began to feel uneasy when the fields of wheat seemed to close in around her.

"Just as well," she told the gim in her best brave voice. "Now no one will see us."

But someone *did* see.

The landing field was lighted up like a little city at night. All that light made the stars vanish and chased away the light of the little slender moon. The field was noisy as a city, too, full of the shouts of *Sojourner*'s crew at work. In the hours since Irdha had been here, a dozen large domes had been erected at the far end of the field. Instant warehouses. Beneath the bright lights, men shoved full anti-gravity pallets from *Sojourner* to the domes as though they were light as balloons. People would come here in the morning to carry away the goods to the city far beyond Great-aunt Iowen's fields.

Irdha kept close to the edge of the wheat field, hiding in the shadows. She crouched down, keeping low and hugging the blue gim hard. She must look for her chance and be ready to slip aboard the ship when no one was looking.

Little by little, *Sojourner* was unloaded, and soon most of the crew were inside one or another of the storage domes. Irdha crept closer, slipping through the shadows. Here the wheat field didn't have a straight edge but went round a bend, for the landing area was wide and circular. Past the bend she'd be behind *Sojourner* and less likely to be seen by anyone in the storage domes.

"All right, gim," she whispered. "We're almost there, and—"

"And," said a voice from ahead, "you'll be on your way home?"

Irdha's breath snagged in her throat. She stopped in her tracks, then turned to run. She didn't get a step before two hands caught her by the shoulders. She turned, shaking, to see Great-aunt Iowen smiling Mom's smile.

Across the landing field a man's voice called out, "Ho! Iowen! Are you ready?"

Great-aunt Iowen waved and shouted that she was. She turned Irdha 'round to face the ship and gave her a little gentle shove. "Let's go, child. I'll give you a hand getting settled."

Irdha nodded, too shaken to speak. She eyed Great-aunt Iowen suspiciously, but Iowen only laughed and guided her across the landing field and up the ramp into *Sojourner*.

"Well!" said Great-aunt Iowen, snapping out a shirt all wrinkled from being stuffed into Irdha's pillowcase. "I suppose you didn't think anyone would follow to help you, did you?"

Irdha nodded, still suspicious.

"Ah, well, I'm not one to keep someone with me by force. If you want to leave, child, then you must leave.

And," she said, answering Irdha's unasked question, "no, I haven't said anything to your father. You know how he is. He'll just insist on keeping you here the way he insisted on taking your mother to Bifrost."

Irdha nodded again, but still carefully. She reached into her sack and pulled out a handful of 3DVid tubes, but her hands were still shaking and she spilled them onto the deck. "Didn't Mom want to go?" she asked, on her knees to gather the tubes.

"Not really. But she loved your father very much and she thought it would be worse to be without him here than to be anywhere in the galaxy with him. That was your mother, very adventurous." Great-aunt Iowen got down on the deck to help collect the tubes. "You're a bit like her, aren't you?"

"I guess so. People say I look like her."

Great-aunt Iowen pursed her lips thoughtfully. "You do. She was a poet, you know."

"I know. Dad says she was full of strange and beautiful ideas."

"She was indeed, and we missed all her songs and poems and stories when she left." She sighed and juggled the 3DVid tubes from one hand to another. "Well, I haven't heard any of those stories in ages, and I don't know a single poem your mother made after she went to live on Bifrost."

"Oh, there were tons of those! Mom was always making one poem or another. They were all about Earth and how much she wanted to come home."

"And when you say 'home' you think of Bifrost, don't you?"

Irdha said it was so.

"Because you were born there?"

Irdha shook her head. It was getting harder to talk now. Her throat was closing up with tears. "No. Because Mom is there."

Great-aunt Iowen was quiet for a long moment, tapping her fingers on her knee. Then she leaned forward and said, "Why do you think your mother is there and not here?"

"Because she is, that's why. She's buried there."

"Your mother died there, yes." Great-aunt Iowen leaned forward and touched one finger to Irdha's chest, right where her heart beat. "But, child, she *lives* here."

Irdha frowned, suspecting a trick, but Great-aunt Iowen only smiled.

"There's an old saying here on Earth, so old no one knows who made it up, but it's so true that people have been saying it for years. 'Home,' they say, 'is where the heart is.' Your mother knew this, and she followed her heart to Bifrost with your father. She knew this, even though she longed to return to Earth one day." She reached out to brush Irdha's fair hair away from her cheek. "That was a powerful longing, so strong that she named you after her homeworld. But your mother's heart was always with her husband and her children. She knew that wherever they were, she would always be home."

Irdha swallowed hard. Suddenly she remembered hearing Dad's gentle snoring and Davy's sleepy sighs. Earlier, they had just been noises to cover the sounds of her escaping footfalls. Now, in her memory, they were the familiar sounds of home transplanted to this alien place.

"I'd miss them," she said, surprised to hear her own voice. She'd only thought she was thinking that.

Great-aunt Iowen smiled gently. "And they would miss you."

Irdha frowned again, for her memory took her farther back than today, to the days aboard *Sojourner* when it had been so hard to talk to Dad and Davy about Mom. She'd felt so shut out then, so alone with her sorrow.

"They wouldn't miss me so much," she said bitterly. "They'd get over me like they've gotten over Mom."

"Hush, child! What makes you think they are 'over' your mother?"

Irdha shrugged. "They don't even talk about her. They never let me talk about her."

Great-aunt Iowen put an arm around her and rocked a little, side to side. "They get all quiet and gruff, don't they? Well, your father's always been like that, so it doesn't surprise me that your brother is, as well. Your mother and I, though—we were different. We could fill the night with our talking. Talking, talking, telling stories, telling hopes, giggling at the moon. We were great talkers."

Then Great-aunt Iowen got briskly to her feet, dusting her hands together exactly the way Mom used to do when she was finished with one chore and ready to start another. "Well, Irdha, it's time for me to go get some sleep. Old farm ladies like me have to get up very early to get all the work done. Now you should know that I've paid the ship's captain for your passage home, so you won't have to hide in a storage locker till you're halfway there. You're all set to go." She bent down and took Irdha's face in her two hands. "Give me a kiss good-bye and I'll be on my way."

Her lips brushed Irdha's cheek. Her hug was strong and warm. Aching filled up Irdha's chest, but not the kind you feel when you're about to cry. It was worse than that, deeper than that. To her surprise, Irdha realized this was the same homesick aching she used to feel whenever she thought about Mom and Bifrost. Now she was feeling it when she thought of leaving Earth and her family!

Irdha listened to Great-aunt Iowen's footfalls on the deck outside the cabin. She heard them grow fainter as they went farther away. The aching in her chest swelled now. Tears welled up in her eyes.

Oh, it wasn't fair! Why couldn't her feelings settle down and decide where home was?

Home, it was said here on this alien world, is where the heart is.

Very quietly, still aching and confused, Irdha followed behind Great-aunt Iowen, tiptoeing down the corridor to where the wide doors stood open to the night. Outside, the wind still whistled, and the lights still glared. Irdha leaned her head far back and thought she was just able to see the faintest bit of lonesome moon beyond the artificial lights.

"All set, Iowen?" called the ship's captain from the foot of the ramp.

"All set," Great-aunt Iowen said, but then she stopped when she felt Irdha's hand in hers. She bent down a little, and she said, "Aren't you ready to go yet, child?"

Yellow lights twinkled in the farmhouse beyond the wheat fields, and Irdha knew—she just knew—that Dad and Davy were up, wondering where she was. Poor Dad! He must be so worried! All of a sudden she wanted to hug him, and to be hugged by him. She wanted that more than anything else.

"I want to go home," she said. She squeezed Great-aunt Iowen's hand. "But I don't really know where home is anymore."

Gently, Great-aunt Iowen said, "Ah, but I think you do."

Irdha swallowed hard, then nodded. She looked away across the wheat to the yellow lights gleaming in the farmhouse windows and even managed a smile.

Seeing that smile, Great-aunt Iowen stood up and called down to the captain. "Jeremy! We have one more bundle to off-load here!"

The captain smiled and waved them down. "Where's it going?"

Irdha looked up into his kind gray eyes, then past him to the little farmhouse far at the edge of the wheat fields where surely her father paced the floors and her brother spoke gruff words of comfort. Now she longed to be with them just as strongly as she'd longed to return to Bifrost.

"Home," she said, smiling. "I'm going home."

ABOUT THE AUTHORS

ARTHUR C. CLARKE is the world-renowned author of such science-fiction classics as *2001: A Space Odyssey*—for which he shared an Oscar nomination with director Stanley Kubrick—and *The Songs of Distant Earth,* as well as over two dozen other books of fiction and nonfiction. He resides in Sri Lanka, where he continues to write and consult on issues of science, technology, and the future.

CONNIE WILKINS lives in the five-college area of western Massachusetts, where she co-owns two stores supplying the nonessential necessities of student life. Her stories have appeared most recently in *Marion Zimmer Bradley's Fantasy Magazine*, the DAW anthology *Prom Night*, and *Bruce Coville's Shapeshifters.*

DAVID R. BUNCH, poet and fiction writer, has kept well out of the limelight in St. Louis while contributing a unique voice to science fiction. His first story appeared in *If* in 1957. Many of the stories he has written were gathered in the novel *Moderan* (1971) and *Bunch* (1993).

ALETHEA EASON lives in Lake County, California, with her husband, Bill. She's had stories published in *Marion Zimmer Bradley's Fantasy Magazine*, *New Moon Magazine*, *Shoofly*, and most recently in the anthologies, *A Glory of Unicorns* and *Bruce Coville's Alien Visitors.*

JOHN C. BUNNELL lives and writes in Oregon. His stories have appeared in a variety of anthologies for children and adults, including *Horrors! 365 Scary Stories,* and *Bruce Coville's Shapeshifters.* The characters in "Free Will," he says, are entirely fictional—at least in this universe.

NINA KIRIKI HOFFMAN has been pursuing a writing career for seventeen years and has sold more than 150 stories, and several novels. She frequently sells short stories to DAW anthologies, *Fantasy and Science Fiction Magazine*, and elsewhere. Nina lives in Eugene, Oregon, with many dolls and cats and a growing animé collection.

JANE YOLEN has published more than 170 books. Her work ranges from the slaphappy adventures of Commander Toad, to such dark and serious novels as *The Devil's Arithmetic* (which was made into a Showtime movie), to the space fantasy of her much-beloved *Pit Dragon Trilogy*. She lives in a huge old farmhouse in western Massachusetts with her husband, computer scientist David Stemple.

ANNE MAZER grew up in a family of writers in upstate New York. Her work includes *The Salamander Room*, *Moose Street*, and *The Oxboy*. Anne lives in Ithaca, New York, with her son, Max, and daughter, Mollie.

NOREEN DOYLE was born in New Jersey and, at the age of eight, moved to Maine, where she had her first contact with an "alien" culture. Although she is an older sister and has degrees in anthropology, she never engages in silent barter unless she is very sure of what she will be getting—and will be giving up in exchange.

GUS GRENFELL is best known by kids in Britain for his soccer stories, poetry, and rock musicals, but he has also had adult SF and fantasy stories published in Britain and the United States. Gus lives on a small hill farm in England's Yorkshire Pennines, with his wife and family and quite a lot of animals.

NICHOLAS FISK is the author of over two dozen science-fiction short stories and books. Among his novels are *Mindbenders*, *A Hole in the Head*, and *Grinny*.

EDMOND HAMILTON was born in Ohio in 1900 and sold his first story to the pulp magazine *Weird Tales* in the late 1920s. Before his death in 1977, he had over three hundred stories published under a variety of names; among his novels are *Sacrifice Hit* and *Babylon in the Sky*. Along with *Lensman* novelist E. E. "Doc" Smith, he is considered to be the co-creator of the action-packed genre known as "space opera."

KAREN JORDAN ALLEN has been many things, including an opera company secretary, divinity student, pianist, and Spanish teacher, and hopes to one day scale Katahdin, the highest mountain in Maine. Another of her stories appears in the anthology *A Nightmare's Dozen*. Karen lives in Maine with her husband and their four-year-old daughter.

NANCY VARIAN BERBERICK has written stories for three other Bruce Coville anthologies: *Ghosts II*, *A Glory of Unicorns*, and *Bruce Coville's Shapeshifters*. Nancy also writes fantasy fiction for grown-ups; her latest novel is *Tears of the Night Sky*. Nancy lives with her husband, architect Bruce A. Berberick, and their two dogs, Pagie and Piper, in Charlotte, NC.

ABOUT THE ARTISTS

ERNIE COLÓN, cover and interior artist, has worked on a wide variety of comic book–related projects during the course of his long career, including graphic novels, comic strips, and various superhero titles. His most current work came in providing the cover paintings for *Bruce Coville's Alien Visitors* and *Bruce Coville's Shapeshifters*, and the interior art for the latter. Ernie lives on Long Island, New York, with his wife and daughter.

JOHN NYBERG, who inked the story illustrations, has been a comic book artist for fourteen years. Among his many accomplishments are *Green Arrow*, *Plastic Man*, and *The Flash* for DC Comics; *Doom 2099* for Marvel; and *WildC.A.T.S.* and *Gen^{13}* for Image. His most recent work was as inker for *Bruce Coville's Alien Visitors* and *Bruce Coville's Shapeshifters*. John lives in New Jersey with his wife, Amy, and their two cats, Bart and Lisa.

BRUCE COVILLE was born in Syracuse, New York, and grew up in a rural area north of the city, around the corner from his grandparents' dairy farm. He lives in a brick house in Syracuse with his wife, his youngest child, three cats, and a dog named Thor. Though he has been a teacher, a toy-maker, and a gravedigger, he prefers writing. His dozens of books for young readers include the bestselling *My Teacher Is an Alien* series, *Goblins in the Castle*, *Aliens Ate My Homework*, and *Sarah's Unicorn*. His most recent work is the book and television series *I Was a Sixth Grade Alien*.